CW01511898

SOMEWHERE IN TIME

James Reynolds Bertel

 iUniverse

SOMEWHERE IN TIME

iUniverse books may be ordered through booksellers or by contacting:

iUniverse
1663 Liberty Drive
Bloomington, IN 47403
www.iuniverse.com
1-800-Authors (1-800-288-4677)

ISBN: 978-1-5320-8487-4 (sc)
ISBN: 978-1-5320-8486-7 (e)

Library of Congress Control Number: 2019916755

Print information available on the last page.

iUniverse rev. date: 10/18/2019

Contents

Epilogues

Frontispiece - Somewhere in Time

Somewhere in time,
One Sunny morn,
We will awaken to find each other again.
Somewhere it will not be too late for us.

Someday we will stroll together
On a quiet afternoon;
On a moon bright night
We will have our dance.

Somewhere in time,
In the light snowfall of Winter,
In a glimmering Spring,
In a shimmering Summer,
In an Autumn of vibrant color.

Where or when we cannot know,
Nor how we will find each other,
But it matters not,
For somewhere I will know your love,
And you, mine.

Somewhere in time.

Author's Note

This story is written in both the first-person and third-person. The first-person chapters and passages are extracts from Bertie's diaries, his letters, or his emails, and they are labeled as such. The poems interspersed were written by Bertie and are referred to in the chapters which they follow. Maps included in certain chapters are the maps used by Bertie in either preparation for, or execution of, his New Guinea Expedition.

The story herein is the story of a man's life, especially the latter part of his life, and his relationship with two women. The story does not pretend to be comprehensive –indeed, his early life features only certain episodes –four from his adolescence, and a few from his wartime service. It is also, in the end, the story of his lonely quest in the wildness of New Guinea, to solve the mystery of a lost aircraft and its crew.

And in the end, it is really the story of a man who followed his conscience and remained true to his Duty, as he saw it.

Dedication

Dedicated to Dale C. McIntyre and Ingrid S. Bertel. Without your unstinting love and inspiration, this work would have never been written.

And to my sister, Leslie Anne Bertel, who always encouraged me to keep writing.

Fenway

"I'd like the memory of me
   to be a happy one.
I'd like to leave an afterglow
      of smiles when life is done…
I'd like the tears of those who grieve,
   To dry before the sun
Of happy memories that I leave
   When life is done."
(for my sister, Leslie Anne Bertel, 1956-2014)

I am left with one overriding imprint on my emotions, bequeathed
to me by Leslie Anne: infectious enthusiasm. In a game we attended
at the hallowed ground of the Boston Red Sox, the revered Fenway
Park, no native-born Bostonian was capable of surpassing the sheer
energy of her response to every pitch thrown. For nine glorious
innings I studied Leslie's mannerisms- a low rumble of grumbling,
impatient and indecipherable string of complaints, punctuated by

volcanic eruptions of utter euphoria with a little as a blooping Texas League single as the catalyst. With the rest of the Red Sox Nation getting to their feet right along with her, I was compelled to stand up so abruptly, so many times, I implored her to let me off the roller coaster ride that greeted you with each and every Red Sox contest at Fenway.

And her veteran enthusiasm at the game carried over into the mad subway ride away from the ball park. She would howl with knowing laughter at every train stop, as more and more departing fanatics were vacuum packed into subway cars long since filled to capacity. The cacophony of voices filled the stagnant air of the train car with every manner of post game analysis imaginable, until every inning had been replayed to their satisfaction.

Strolling back to our hotel, after pushing our way through our fellow sardines to exit the train, my little sister recounted over and over a solid, rising line drive leaving the bat of "Big Papi", David Ortiz himself, and vanishing into the throng of spectators packing the right-center field bleachers. On this night, Ortiz' four-bagger sealed a Sox victory over the tenacious Seattle Mariners. Nearing the hotel, she softly hummed, then loudly sang "Sweet Caroline", the seventh-inning stretch theme of the now World Champions.

Despite the indelible stamp she left upon me that summer evening in Boston, I will remember my little sister best in quieter moments, and it was such times I finally realized what she should be remembered for most of all- her elemental humanity and humaneness. These twin blessings she brought to her dealings with all she came into contact with, whether a stray dog or a human being who had strayed from the Right Path.

And now she is gone. I am left not with emptiness because she is forever absent from my life. No, I stand here on this earth a proud man. In those quiet moments, I am most touched by her; and I now hear her voice telling me one final thought, a fitting wrap-up to that magical night at Fenway: she said to me "You know, Jim, I really love those people. The people we saw tonight, the ones in the subway".

Her words come suddenly to me now in the stillness of quiet moments, and I know now what she did with her life:

She loved.

Preface

AUTUMN PASSAGE

The air is crisp again. Again, a twist of fate comes around. Another October, another chance to speak his mind. He had been struck by her physical beauty years before. And now? The beauty of her soul, that which lay inside her began to seep into him. Glances at each other in years past now made a cruel sense, cruel because of the years that had been lost. In response to a series of his inevitable compliments on her appearance she said to him: "I don't yet know what I want."

Telling someone how you have been affected by them, that they may have been injected into your very veins: Must these feelings remain unspoken? High regard; and surprisingly a rapidly overtaking and deepening mutual ease together. Must these forever remain prisoners in their hearts? Thoughts without a voice?

It will not be so this time, he declared to himself. When you go away, marching off again in a forlorn quest of another Grail…this time, he promised, you shall not do so in silence. They were as two ships, lonely ships on the sea that pass in the night. Will they stop, even for a single moment in time and exchange the boon of love and embrace on a long, lonely passage, a passage of otherwise bereft of true happiness? Who can divine what fate awaits them? To reverse course is folly. To pass with but a greeting is cold. To stop even for a relatively brief time: perhaps to exchange the gift of love, a gift not ephemeral but eternal. Lighting the utter darkness, bringing the warmth and tenderness; a stillness of contentment, an escalating sense of peace spreading over them. Will they hold each other? And ever so gently, hold on to each other through the night.

The twilight of Morn breaks through, the night gives way. In the East the sun begins its climb. Did the night bring them together in an unstained Peace? To him any disappointment would be tempered by this: now and forever he would keep her in his heart. Would she keep him in hers?

O. B. T.

It struck him, now a gangly, enthusiastic fifteen-year-old, as exciting. His father had been alert with SAC, the Strategic Air Command. But this was not usual, as any Air Force Brat could tell you, for at all times fifty percent of Aircrew were on Alert. These airmen were ensconced in their alert bunkers on the flight line. Only this time, ALL aircrew were not on alert, they had been instructed to be in their aircraft at their stations: and his father's station was the left-hand pilot's seat in a KC-135 aerial tanker. All 916 tankers in the United States were manned, as were the entire operational force of B-52 bombers, and their bomb bays carried nuclear weapons.

He had watched in the days before the President speaking to the country and placing a naval quarantine around the island of Cuba. It would later be called the Cuban Missile Crisis. What excited the boy was his father coming home driven by an NCO in a blue pickup in the middle of the alert. Apparently, they all released in shifts to drive to base housing to warn their families to get ready. The boy's mother went straight out to greet him. There was no small talk. The Pilot told his wife in short, clipped tone, to pack the family station wagon with water and canned goods, radios, batteries and so forth and stay by the telephone and if she received a phone call from him to pack the kids up and head to the nearby Sierra Nevada mountains.

Then the Pilot embraced his three children, stood back up and the boy watched his parents embrace briefly. A quick kiss and he was gone. The boy could not know what his parents knew: that they were probably saying good bye for the last time. His father knew that if he got the order to take off, even if he survived his mission, there would be nothing to come back to.

The boy watched the blue pickup vanish around the corner. He watched his mother from inside the front door screen. Her gaze was fixed on the now vacant corner for a moment, then she bowed her head to her chest, then raised her head. She brought Tinkerbelle the family dog inside then stayed on the porch for a brief time. The boy watched her carefully, saying nothing. He noticed she wore an expression of almost hollow sadness. He knew at once, seeing her drawn and pained face, then a brief clear vision of his father's and placing the two side by side, that was not exciting at all. Placing the two faces side by side, he saw the grimness in them. He saw that the two of them shed no tears—it was enough, the closeness, the furrows of a desperate sadness gave way to an ease of manner, of remembered fondness, of a time long ago and far away. Later, after both of his parent's lives were over, he found among their things exactly when and where they had communed in another crisis in their lives.

He found four words penciled on a dirty corner of a V-Mail envelope, four words that said all they ever needed to retain hope. He thought of the date: January 1945, those words written in another time of travail and near-heartbreak. Perhaps they were written in Chabua, his base in India, more likely Lungling or some other desolate Chinese Airfield. Sixty missions in sixty days, flying Chinese troops to plug the leaks springing up the length of Central China, as the Japanese closed in on the exhausted Flyer's aerodromes. He saw in his mind a man, his father, fighting to remain unbroken. On the run, only just barely beyond the grasp of the surging Japanese, he had penciled the words on that corner of the V-Mail envelope.

His mother would read the laconic message. Her brother had been missing now for three months, somewhere in the Pacific. She knew the scrap of envelope in her hands, and it's at once brave and fearful code letters, meant her husband's last reserves had been reached.

The few carefully penciled words were: Until O. B. T.
Orange Blossom Time.

None But The Lonely Heart

(an extract from Bertie's Diary)
"None but the lonely heart
Can know my sorrow,
Alone and parted
Far from my joy and gladness,
Heaven's boundless arch I see
Spread out above me…"
    -P. Tchaikovsky (based on a poem by J.W. Goethe)

The Cuban Missile Crisis was over. No mission was flown by my Father. And none too soon, for we were transferred to another Strategic Air Command Base in Maine-from Mather in California to Loring on the Canadian border in northern Maine.

At fifteen years old, I was to be dropped off in December at my Grandparents' home in Gibbstown, New Jersey to finish my Sophomore year of high school. It would be my third high school, a condition common to Air Force Brats following their Fathers around the country or the world in a gypsy life every 3-4 years. I would attend the same high school that my mother and her brother James attended. I was my Uncle Jim's namesake. He had vanished in a B-24 bomber in 1944, and all of my young life was inculcated with this memory.

My Grandfather was also named James. Later, when my progenitors were long gone, I would read Grandpa's diary. From his entries for 1938, perhaps the most fulfilling of his life, I realized that he had arranged my detour on the way to Maine. His son was also 15 in 1938. I guess it was sort of reliving of that year for Grandpa-to take me under his wing, teach me; it was as if he longed to steer me to manhood in the shadow of Uncle Jim.

He was, during the first months together, to lift his curtain of silence about his son. On April 28th, Uncle Jim's birthday (they called him Buddy), we two sat quietly in the drawing room. Above the fireplace mantle where the portraits of Mom and Uncle Jim I had so often seen. He looked directly at these and, in a thickening voice, said "You know Jim, it is at times like these I miss him the most".

From that moment I saw Grandpa as a man with a corner of his soul scarred with a wound, never to heal. Randomly, since that excruciating day of the Western Union telegram, the scar would ache and throb until he thought he could bear no more, then fade. It would never leave him.

And so, with this abrupt realization, I now share that ache, not as a literal and physical and mental cold hand on my heart, but in a figurative sense. Because this acute anguish was new to me, it was all that more branded into my memory. My great respect for him was now wedded to a new determination to stand by him at all costs, forbidding any intrusion into our communal bond.

It was enough that day for us to simply sit quietly. I knew somehow, he was waiting for my inquiries about his Boy. And so, began my questions, hesitant at first. They were never to end, and Grandpa answered them with fair detail. But only sufficient knowledge I could easily absorb, and probably only that detail which he could impart while remaining steady.

Years later in his papers I would find the Western Union telegram, from the War Department, telling him his son was missing in action. I saw it had been addressed to HIM and not to my Grandmother, and it was delivered at the DuPont plant where he worked. I visualized him opening it at the plant, at 2:30 in the afternoon, and I cringed at thinking of his utter anguish. Then he must have thought of how he was going to tell his wife and daughter. My mother was home my father was overseas as well, in India and China. In those papers too were my Uncle's personal effects, shockingly few. There were two photographs. One was of his dog, Queenie, a Fox Terrier, the other was of the front of the house where he had longed to be. Uncle Jim had written on the back: "Up this walk, someday..." Seeing this sentiment and what my Grandfather had written below these words broke my heart. He was a father reading the longing words of a son who was gone forever. Grandpa wrote: "But he never made it back from the Southwest Pacific".

I would accumulate the story in my mind for many years. I did not know that many years later I would finally set off in search of Uncle Jim, his crew mates, and his aircraft: PHOTO QUEEN. That journey was to end in the swamps, jungles, and mountains of far off New Guinea coast.

Ten years after my time with Grandpa, I myself returned from another war. One day I studied a map of the Southwest Pacific. Now comparing the story of Uncle Jim's fatal flight to the map, tracing the last known position of the aircraft on a direct line to the New Guinea coast.

My finger came to rest near the spot to which I was to journey 40 years later. I immediately appraised Grandpa of my theory in person. I saw him light up when I told him I wanted to go there and look around. It was a promise I never fulfilled in his lifetime, or even my mother's lifetime, much to my discredit and shame.

But finally, after 40 years, I was to keep my word to him. And I would be sitting on that coast imagining the roar and the blue exhaust flames, the B-24 passing overhead and on into the darkness inland. Somewhere in that darkness, I thought, somewhere...

I would speak aloud to him: Grandpa I'm here. Here where he died.

A little late.
Just a little late.

Once Upon A Time

If I should die,
Think only this of me:
That while I lived,
I lived for thee. -Quatrain, a poem written for Jonie by Bertie.

All the way up to this time, his last year in high school, he had no luck with the opposite sex. Actually, because of a painful shyness, he had hardly tried to have any luck with the opposite sex. His last two years of high school were spent playing baseball and soccer and sticking by his closest friend, Jack. As a matter of fact, the two of them were loners. Polite and affable with their classmates, they nonetheless stuck together in all that they did. They did not mix much with their classmates.

Jonie entered his life in the spring semester of their senior year in high school. During the previous year he had observed her from afar, typically too shy to approach her at all. He had been struck by her personality, a vivacious one, and he regarded her as beautiful. He could not know that one night in the spring of that year would launch seven more years of association, good and bad, with Jonie. It would in fact become almost an obsession that consumed him. But now the full flush of youth ha had approached her and engaged in conversation, and it was this initial opening that led her to inviting him to a spring dance at the social club for the school. The only catch was: Jonie already had a boyfriend. She had invited him to accompany both of them to the dance. Being star struck he accepted, despite the warning from Jack that it was no good. But he was blinded by the excitement of being with her and at his first attended dance since he was a freshman in high school back in California three years before.

The event proceeded uneventfully, he alone with his thoughts or in conversation with Jonie. After two hours her boyfriend, fed up with not being paid attention to much, left the two alone and mixed with the other kids. Bertie tried to continue small talk with her but, failing in that he became silent.

After what seemed like a long period of silence, Jonie drew up to him, her face in front of his. She closed the gap quickly and kissed him. Then she drew back, smiled, and asked him if he had liked his kiss, to which query he was only capable of stammering out a Yes. In truth he had been thunderstruck. It was if he had been launched into the cold night sky. He fell for her at once; and he fell hard. He could hardly believe what had just happened. The days and evenings following would find him sitting on her front steps, the two of them engaged in earnest conversation, many times in earnest debate over some radical idea that had germinated in his mind. He found he could not possibly win these arguments. A superb debater on the school team, he was helpless to do anything but capitulate in subject surrender to her will. Despite the small detail that she retained her boyfriend, he was consumed by love for her. In fact, it was Jonie's bout with Tonsillitis that launched his consuming interest in Medicine and would lead him years later to attain a career as a physician.

But graduation would separate them, he off to a military academy with Jack and she to a civilian college out West. As the day of departure for them approached, he became afflicted by sadness beyond anything experienced before. They agreed to correspond, at his urging.

As he departed for the Academy, he could not imagine what that pledge would lead to. He knew only one thing: in his heart he knew that one day they would be together and stay together for a lifetime. To him, it was ordained. To him it was the Right outcome. Thoughts of any other future were banished from his mind.

He would not know how wrong he was, and that he would be devastated by the failure of his fondest aspiration.

* * *

Separated by 2,000 miles, Bertie and Jonie would not see each other again for five years. Bertie bombarded her with correspondence amounting to two or three letters per month. Jonie replied with but a handful of letters, one of them reeking of perfume, and all of the ending with the appellation Love, Jonie and four X's representing kisses. But Bertie was caught up in Academy sports and studies, and summer's spent in military training; and Jonie was frequently away at summer school. Nevertheless, Bertie never wavered in his love for her nor the absolute belief the two of them were destined to marry.

He and his Cadet classmates came to regard the Academy as akin to prison. Severe hazing was dealt out to them during their Fourth Class (Plebe) year. During the ten months of this crucible, fifteen of his classmates in their assigned Company quit, leaving a hard core of twenty Cadets, who three years later would graduate with their degrees and commissions as Lieutenants in the armed services.

Upon graduation Bertie began his assignments to various training stations of the United States Marine Corps. Correspondence with Jonie slackened but never stopped. With his assignment to the Defense Language Institute in Monterey to study Vietnamese, he managed to reunite with Jonie, who was attending college in San

Jose. They would spend a couple of uneventful weekends together. But it was not until nine months later that he managed to see her again, spending a crisp fall weekend at her parent's home in Virginia. Bertie had just received his orders to be shipped overseas to Vietnam. He had only four days Leave, and he flew back East to say a quick goodbye to his own mother and father. Then he hastened down to see Jonie in Virginia. It was a disaster to him from start to finish. The two of them took a drive on a beautiful Autumn Saturday in the countryside. Mostly casual conversation ensued, and the shy Bertie as usual said little. Until, that is, he blurted out to her that he loved her. At this, Jonie abruptly told him to pull over, and as soon as he stopped the car Jonie leaned over quickly and began kissing him- hard, frenzied, full kisses that startled him. There was no tenderness in her sudden assault as she pulled away from and asked him in an angry voice if he now felt any different. Bertie, shocked at what had just happened, could only reaffirm his love for her. She seemed exasperated at his words. That evening she apologized to him. But he knew now there was little hope left. In front of the house the next day they stood formally apart to say goodbye. Bertie mustered enough courage to ask her to "wait for me". She turned him down, in as kind a way she could manage, but it was his last desperate appeal, and now it was denied. They promised each other to write, but this he knew was just a token gesture. She gave him that wonderful smile he so much longed to see. Then he drove off, and as he did, he felt broken inside, opening the windows and letting the blast of cold air wash over him.

*   *   *

(three years later)

A man, a woman and a baby sat in a booth in a Virginia coffee shop waiting to order. The man was dressed in the uniform of a Marine officer. The baby was not his; the woman was married to another man. The waitress took their orders, then the man asked the woman if they shouldn't get the infant a "grilled cheese sandwich or something". The waitress rolled her eyes and laughed and said to the woman "he doesn't know much about babies, does he. You are going to have to teach him!", and the waitress left. The man and woman sat looking at each other in silence. Then in a gentle, measured voice she said to him "For years I ran around with a lot of guys never knew what they wanted. And the man who did know what he wanted was right there in front of me the entire time". Saying nothing, he simply turned his head to the window and let his gaze come to rest on the tops of the trees outside. The trees were gently swaying in the warm breeze of summer.

The two of them parted in the parking lot. They would never see each other again.

Ghosts

(abandoned Loring AFB, Maine)

Bertie, Black Jack, and Jack's lovely wife Celeste drove straight down the runway. Starting near the Outer Marker off the end of the runway, they began a straight-line journey down a concrete thoroughfare where B-52 bombers and KC-135 aerial tankers once rolled into takeoff runs. On past the now vacant Alert Bunkers where their fathers once waited for the possibly dreaded call for pilots to man their aircraft. Past the massive repair hanger and finally beyond the silent control tower, abandoned so many years ago.

Bertie thought of his father, scrambling into Alert vehicle that would deliver him and his Crew to a Tanker with engines already lit off and running. The ear-splitting Alert Siren would be sounding the tocsin to another Drill or to War. Jackson conjured up his father in his imagination-as Base Fire Chief sitting patiently in a lead vehicle of the Crash Party, his engines lined up in formation off his flank.

Since the Strategic Air Command (SAC) demanded it, one half of all air crew at all times would spend fifty percent of their existence

15

on Alert status, living in those bunkers. Bertie reflected that, as a boy growing up on air bases, it was a natural thing to have his father gone 50% of the time. Now, passing as if in Review past all the abandoned detritus of an era now consigned to history, and with both their parents gone, emotion welled up in both men. Bertie saw in his mind's eye a jet aircraft, his father's Tanker, belching black exhaust smoke as it accelerated down the runway, directly in front of him and bearing down on his car. Then it lifts off, passing just overhead with a deafening roar, its bright aluminum fuselage flashing in the sun; and then it is behind him- with an ever-steepening upward angle, the great jet claws for attitude. The aircraft grows smaller and smaller, then vanishes into a cottony white cumulus cloud mass. "On and up, up into the delirious burning blue" Bertie says to himself, remembering the imagery from the poem: high Flight". Like the pilot-poet who wrote it, his father had just broken free of the surly bonds of earth.

They then cut off the flight line and paraded past the Base Exchange, commissary, movie theater and bowling alley and social club set up for them as kids. The three of them stopped at the infamous Water Tower, representing for Jack and Bertie the Mt. Everest of their youth. They had climbed it one spring night in their senior year-all the way to its pinnacle, frighteningly close to slipping off its slick surface. Once atop the summit, they would sit triumphantly on the single drain pipe protruding into the cool night air, two hundred feet up.

For Bertie, this place brought back the memory of Jonie. Forty years had passed, yet she still haunted him. They passed down the streets of housing where they once lived. Jack had lived on the same street as Jonie, but here the houses had all been bulldozed and were now gone, right around the corner from Bertie's former residence. He remembered happily mounting his bicycle and, turning the corner, his spirits would soar as he sped down to see her. This current trip triggered in him once again thoughts of what had gone wrong between them. Those thoughts tortured him even after he had returned home. He saw his wife as his salvation from this torment, but she remained distant from him. She just figuratively had slammed the door in his face.

He did not yet know that only two months hence he was to be lifted out of his circle of hell by someone he only knew casually. That someone was Claire.

Comrades

He was struck immediately by the enthusiasm with which these schoolmates of long ago greeted each other, and the recounting of their years since. And by their assumption of an easy and altogether comfortable manner with each other, and which they effortlessly fell into almost at once.

More than just friends really; that term seemed wholly inadequate. The bond between them was forged from their commonality: raised in the Gypsy lives of their families, all shared the two faces of constant uprooting of the homestead: new and thrilling vistas opened up to them, tempered by the pain of associations closed off forever. But the High School years, the final crucible of their adolescence, would be intimately shared with each other. A commune was thus formed- a voluntary one in which all tasks and rewards were divided equally according to the abilities of each. And each gave the others their hand when someone flagged. They were Comrades in Arms, struggling together against the "slings and the arrows" of their teenage travails, guided by their sometimes bemused, sometimes incredulous parents and teachers.

They reveled in the retelling of their tales of petty delinquencies. And the strict discipline imposed as a result by their seemingly unforgiving parents. There was initially a gulf separating two groups of the class: the Air Force Brats and the kids who had made the small town their home their entire lives to date, but what might have been unbridgeable chasm was rapidly, almost imperceptibly filled in by the farmer's sons' and daughters' curiosity and natural hospitality and the revolutionary zeal which marked the new interlopers' fiber of their being. The shy ones of either group were treated with the unfailing courtesy and easygoing embrace of the more vivacious among them. Thus, even he, a painfully shy loner, fell instantly under the spell of their polite smiles and outgoing greetings.

Whether a hero or heroine of the playing fields of glory or an intellectual genie, or anything in between really, the distinctions of merit or social class were erased ruthlessly by the camaraderie that blossomed in their few years together. Of course, academic or athletic merit was given due honor. But those so blessed with talents denied others, never lorded their prowess over their Comrades.

Thusly, they passed an exceedingly pleasant few days together again; sadly, perhaps for the last time.

And so now, ensconced once more in that fabled land of youth, were they blossomed and grew into the first stages of manhood and womanhood, they, not at all surprisingly, sat and conversed and laughed and remembered together what had been the best years of their very young lives. Some were missing, gone forever, but never forgotten: the memory of them permanently cherished by all the others. Those unable to appear dispatched their tales of growth and best wishes to their compatriots. The group of girls (women now, yes, yet he would always remember them as the young girls they once were) banded together and produced a miracle of food, drink, and of course graced the men with a gentle active presence.

And then came the final moments together. To a person, they were not capable of giving that final fare-thee-well without the pangs of emotion lancing into their hearts. A book of memories, produced as out of thin air by those wonderful girls, would be read and reread by them all from time to time. These men and women, forever young for those few days together, then scattered as if blown by capricious winds- just the way it had happened fifty years before.

And just then, they parted with a sure sense of having been blessed and enriched by just having known each other.

None of them, to a person, was capable of giving that final fare-thee-well without some anguish. You could see it in their faces, wistful and thoughtful at the same time. All knew they were now closer to the end rather than the beginning.

Yet for those few days they were, yes that was it: forever young.

Thousand Yard Stare

You pass them in the street each day. They blend into the crowd, nondescript, and unnoticed. Nothing much separates them from all the others. Their banter and conversation are not unlike any number of people in some gathering, and any diverse group of people. And they have the same frowns and smiles as anyone else, the same moods whether downcast or joyful. They are as cordial and polite or as rude and indifferent as anyone. You can find them walking along busy city avenues, in a quiet park, in subways and on country roads. Nothing in particular seems to set them apart. They may be old or young, well off or down on their luck.

But, sometimes, if you look closely, you will see the difference. Not by their skin color, or dress, or by the way they may amble along. If you look at their eyes, then you will never forget them.

They seem to be fixed on someone or something, perhaps they appear to be staring at you.

Yet their eyes see nothing of the sort; there is a vacancy about them. And you may realize, suddenly, their gaze, that vacant stare, is fixed on nothing. They are far away; they are seeing forever. In those

few brief moments that will haunt them from time to time, you will know who they are. Give them a silent thank you. And remember those forever young men who are not with them now. Remember them this way:
"When you go home, tell them of us
And say to them:
For your tomorrow
We gave our today." *
*inscription by Charles Edmonds on the gate of Kohima Cemetery, Assam, India.

Steal Away

"And the night shall be filled with music,
And the cares that infest the day
Shall fold their tents, like the Arabs,
And as silently steal away"-from "The Day is Done" by HW
Longfellow

Marines had filed in a company-long column into the perimeter of
the rear fire base,

And then bivouacked on the open ground on the south side, just
short of the single runway.

Dried mud crusted utilities, matted hair, mangled disintegrating
cigarettes-all these adorned their bodies. They were tired, no-more
than Bertie mused to himself. Not just tired, they were weary, a
weariness of the soul. They flopped down, many of them. Some of
them let themselves down to the ground slowly, with a grown or
curse.

Bertie dug out his poncho-liner, spread it out and, with a sigh of
relief, sat down heavily. After a time just staring vacantly out into the

darkness, he drew a pencil stub and a piece of half-crumpled paper from his utility shirt pocket. By the light of a waxing gibbous moon he began to write. Date, place, then Dear Jonie. He suddenly stopped, his mind really a blank. He tried four times to start the letter, but it was useless. Finally, he just put the pencil and scrap paper down. It came home to him he had had enough. Four months and no letter. She really just doesn't care at all about you, he thought to himself. Not a single letter since he shipped out. Then he cursed softly and lay down heavily on his back, stuffing pencil and crumpled paper back into the shirt pocket. He realized his flak jacket still weighed him down, so he shed that as well as his pistol belt.

Somewhere to the West illumination shells burst in air with their blinding, brightest of whites, magnesium igniting. The parachutes of the flares held them motionless for a second or two, then the burning magnesium torches drifted ever so slowly down, and they winked out into some far-off jungle canopy. To the North heat lightning soundlessly sparked for an instant and vanished. Above him Bertie stared into the fields of palisading stars, sparkling points of white marching deeper and deeper to…? Infinity, he said to himself. A meaningless word. His mind raced for a few moments-beyond the boundary of a finite universe lay nothingness. Another undefinable term. Absolute Truth? Was there such a thing? For 7 years now, for him, Truth was Jonie, the right thing was Jonie and he together, nothing else made any sense to him. Now? He shrank from thinking any longer. To hell with it, he cursed quietly again.

Bertie for just a moment wanted to call out to her. He whispered her name. He tried and tried to see her face, but it would not be yielded up from his memory.

He could no longer see her face.
He began to sink into the morphia of blessed sleep.
She was gone.
Jonie was gone.

Mercy

"The quality of mercy is not strained;
It droppeth as the gentle rain from heaven
Upon the place beneath: it is twice blest,
It blesseth him that gives and him that takes...
It is enthroned in the hearts of kings...-from" Mercy" by William
Shakespeare

He was far beyond reclamation. His abdominal wound was mortal.
The Corpsman had already pronounced it to be so. He was his enemy.
But the Lieutenant sat down in front of him, off the trail, hidden by
foliage from his men. On the trail the men waited. Post security on
the trace he told the sergeant. He rummaged in his small pack and
came out producing a can of peaches, opened it and handed it to the
boy, who tried to gulp greedily down the sweet syrup. His chest was
wracked with spasms of a hacking cough. The lieutenant patiently
made him sip at the can until the syrup was gone.

The men were startled by a muffled gunshot. The lieutenant
emerged from the jungle back onto the trail, placing his .45 back

into a shoulder holster. He and the sergeant looked at each other for a moment, then the lieutenant nodded, and the sergeant softly called out to move. And they all quietly took their places and slipped in silence down the trace.

Forty years later, for him, the quality of mercy is strained. It does not fall in a gentle rain; it comes in a torrent. And he was not the king.

He had stood not in awe, but in shame.

Back To The World

Three days to go. Then the big bird back to the World. That's what they called it: going home. Back to the world. Three days.

The skipper called him in:

Lieutenant you're going to take out one more patrol. Ambush. The lieutenant groaned, then replied, "Yes sir, just give me the dope on it".

So, he takes them out, out through the wire after dark. Dark of the Moon. But not all of them: the rookie kids, the FNGs; the married men, he told them all to stay put.

No more letters he thought, to parents or wives.

They hump to the ambush position, they filter in, and wait. Wait for somebody to come along. They spring it, smoke'em; get back. All through the night they waited, eyes wide. Pupils blown open. Sweating, letting the mosquitoes drink their fill. Just like a dozen times before, except this time: nothing. No hapless enemy comes along. No more letters.

The night of the last day; O'Keefe comes to see him.

Sir I, I don't know what to do when I get back what to tell the folks when I get back. He ran his words out real quick. O'Keefe's eyes are cast down looking at the dirt. He shifts from one foot to the other. This kid is a nervous wreck, the Lieutenant realizes. So, he lights a cigarette, gives one to the boy.

"O'Keefe, you tell them nothing. You get back, take off that uniform, put it in the closet somewhere, and never open that closet again. Then go out and make a life for yourself."

The lieutenant stubbed out the cigarette butt and lay back down.

As things turned out, the Lieutenant would never follow his own advice.

A Walk In The Sun

The Mission, probably the Mission of his life, dropped into Bertie's lap out of the blue. He had purchased a computer on a dare from his son (before this he had routinely damned computers). At a loss with the new device, he typed in his Uncle's name. What he read on the website that popped up stunned him. All his life he had been told, and so the family believed, that his Uncle along with the entire crew of their B-24 bomber had perished in the Southwest Pacific Ocean when the aircraft went down at sea. The plane had disappeared in a Typhoon on September 30, 1944 on the return trip after a mission to the Philippines. Their base was located on Biak Island, which lay off the coast of Northwest New Guinea. The base heard their last radio call at 6:55 pm that evening. The call was a "Mayday". The Photo Queen, as the crew had named it, was never heard from again.

Bertie read in disbelief how the Army had known since 1945 that the Photo Queen had made it to New Guinea coast and, probably out of gas, had crash-landed along the Verkam River, near a town called Sarmi. The story related three investigations after the War by Allied forces had failed to find any of the crew or any trace of the aircraft. Officers of the Japanese forces gave information about the crash to their Allied interrogators after the war ended. These officers admitted that two crew had been captured and executed by beheading. They even named the two captives- one was the copilot and the other a gunner. Bertie's Uncle was the Radio Operator. The Japanese also revealed that the rest of the crew had been killed in gunfights with Japanese troops. Thus, all eleven-crew remained Missing in Action.

Bertie began researching the story and it became almost an obsession, he felt he had to somehow get at the truth. And he shamefully recalled his unfulfilled pledge to his Grandfather so many years ago. During his queries he met a Chicago attorney, Paul, whose Uncle was the executed Gunner. Paul had been researching the mystery of Photo Queen for ten years, tipped off by the same website story Bertie had discovered. Now partners in the quest for truth, they amassed data from countless Archives in the United States, Australia and Holland.

Bertie, tired of research, had come to the decision: he would go to New Guinea and find the answers he needed.

New Guinea. SARMI, MATEWAR, AMSIRA, the VERKAM, the tribes of ISIRAWA, KWERBA, and the unknown AIR MATI, who dwelled on the River of Death. Names that have a sinister ring. Eleven men, kids from towns and farms across the country passed their last days then hours of their lives in these places. And dark and sinister places they became, for them.

70 years had passed. So, he would go there, and he would sit on the beach where his Uncle Jim and his friends died fighting the Japanese.

He would say I am here at last grandpa, a little late but here nonetheless, at last, where your son died. Thus, he would redeem his pledge to his grandfather of 38 years ago. He would keep his Word after all.

He had made the decision in a flash. There was nothing for it but to go. If the remains were there, he would give it all he had left in the tank: keep your eye on the ball they always told him.

It's a gamble he told himself; but you've gotta roll the dice, high stakes: what are the odds? Of finding them 80/20? Maybe? Of getting back? 50/50, not bad. "Where you going', Slick?", was the habitual, mocking question asked of a group of Marines leaving the perimeter to carry out a patrol, by those staying behind the defensive razor wire. The answer: "Just out for a walk in the Sun, Mac." He counted up the ways to rolls snake eyes: the corrupt police, the so-called police boys, the resistance guerrillas, the tribes: bow and arrow types, wolly-bully boys, head hunters, suspected witches burned at the stake. Malaria (tertiary, quartan, cerebral), typhus, Dengue, tularemia, tropical ulcers, leeches, white and red mangrove swamps, sea snakes, swamp snakes, crocodiles, the feared Death Adder maybe. They tend to add up, he thought. Well, maybe, just maybe he would pull it off. You never know, he thought, you just never know.

Claire

"She took me by complete surprise. I sat in dazed astonishment one day, not so long ago. Whether intentional or not, she blind-sided me like a locomotive going full throttle. Right over the edge and into free-fall I went- yet I enjoyed the fall all the way down. Now that I've hit bottom, it is my earnest hope that she will pick me up and put me back together again. And I think she is doing just that, piece by piece. She has awakened in me virtues I had long thought of as dead: a happy, care-free disposition suddenly takes hold of me; an engaging conversationalist appears in place of an irascible hermit; all traces of bitterness, ambivalence and indifference have been erased. She has restored my thirst for life. Laughter and smiles grace my countenance, replacing the brooding, and gruff and silent man I had become. I had hated the man I had become, and Claire had done nothing less than restore the man I used to be; she effortlessly brought out all the best in me. I was now clear-headed, happy-go-lucky, and unruffled by the circumstances of life. She performed this miraculous transformation in only a few weeks, after coming to work for me as a new receptionist.

Of course, we were thrown together every day. I watched in amazement her rapid and energetic organization of the office. My examination rooms suddenly were spotless, the kitchen gleamed with cleanliness, everything now had been put in its proper place in those exam rooms. Her instinct was sure and right on target. I finally blurted out to her one morning that she was the "perfect woman"- beautiful, efficient, and an excellent mother to boot. And then I asked her to become my Private Secretary and Personal Assistant. This was for the simple reason that I had always needed such a woman to remind me of everything. My own short-term memory had been in a shambles since my accidental traumatic brain injury the year before. I was taken aback once more by her rapid, efficient style. It was after I pronounced her to be a perfect woman for the second time that she told me something I never understood. She said, "I do not yet know what I want". It puzzles me to this day.

I had known her only in a formal, casual way for fifteen years. A friend of my wife Carolina, I only occasionally saw her when they got together at our home every few weeks. I admired her physical attributes- she was a stunning green-eyed blonde- but when she left the house, I thought no more about her. We had seldom spoken together at all, just small talk when we were alone waiting for Carolina to come downstairs. I remember only that she had always fixed me with a peculiar stare, wide-eyed and unblinking, as if she were in awe of me. I always did wonder what she was really thinking as she trained those beautiful eyes on me. She seemed to be nervous in my presence.

As my Private Secretary she at once began to orchestrate my affairs with aplomb, and this soon evolved into running my life: Haircuts, car washes, all appointments, all paperwork forms to be done, essential shopping for office supplies, right down to obtaining the proper alcoholic beverages for any weekend guests. Claire instituted weekly briefings in my private office to review the upcoming schedule. It was after these briefings that I began to share with her pieces of writing or poetry that I found compelling.

She always sat and listened to me, giving her undivided attention to my recitations. She seemed to enjoy them and even expressed joy in some of them, emitting a little cry of pleasure as I read, or she even became excited at hearing some of them; and she would abruptly lean all the way across my desk to get a look at what I had just read. My happiness at these moments overcame me, to at last find, in her, someone who appreciated beautiful literature. But it was when I interfered in the routine of the front office that I discovered another trait of Claire's. In one incident she took me back to the inner office, sat me down, and smacked me in the back of the head, and told me in no uncertain terms to stay out of her way. Afterwards I asked her if she were angry with me. She said no, but you will know it when I do get angry with you! After the blow fell, I was surprised to find myself smiling, while I rubbed the back of head. I thought to myself, good Lord, she has changed me overnight. Quite a woman. Yes, quite a woman."- extract from Bertie's diary.

Bertie had begun another of his flirtations. And this with a married woman with three young children. Another harmless dalliance he thought. His innate, and at times, crippling shyness made them benign. He never fell in love; he just enjoyed his few excursions into nothing more than suggestive talk with women, all the while maintaining the half-joking repartee that ensued, inoffensive and self-limiting in every instance. He could not know that this time, all that would change. All he knew was the September sea change in his personality had liberated him and she had bestowed upon him a virtual Renaissance, a rebirth of a long-suppressed volcanic mind- voracious reading, hatching new ideas and schemes, absorbing eclectic knowledge, resuming his single-minded obsession with the pursuit of perfection in the game of golf, renewing his engagement with family and friends. But more than anything else it ignited in him once again the inspiration he needed to begin writing again. Essays, diary entries, short stories, letters, emails, all began to flow. He didn't pause to consider publication; he simply cranked them out.

One project had first claim on his spare time and energy: the by now all-out pursuit of the truth of the loss of the aircraft Photo Queen and its crew. During his research, started in June, he had been introduced to Paul, a Chicago attorney, who's Uncle was also on board the lost plane. They were put in touch with each other by a reclusive Connecticut man who had amassed data about the Crew's squadron. Paul later told Bertie that the man was most likely a former intelligence agent or analyst, who lived in self-imposed obscurity, doling out information to them piece by piece, but never disclosing everything he knew. In any case, Bertie had already made up his mind to go to New Guinea personally and get at the truth. He set his departure date as the following September, began his physical conditioning, and the collection of practical intelligence on the geography, inhabitants, and economy of the island, and the two men delved into archives in America, Australia, Japan, and Holland for clues. Paul amassed thousands of pages of documents and waded through them. As the months wore on, he culled out information that would be critical to Bertie's chances. Bertie became an expert on the tribes he would encounter, memorized the maps, and absorbed the history and political situation in New Guinea, besides committing to memory Paul's treasure trove of documents.

Claire threw herself into the organizing of the mountain of paper. She and Bertie spent hours each week cataloging everything. She also told Bertie categorically "You will never get on that plane to go. You can play with your friends all you want, but we both know you're not going anywhere". Just my intuition, she said. But she never slackened her pace in putting everything he had in order. His wife scoffed at what she saw as just his latest scheme among many. As the months passed Carolina realized he was in dead earnest, and she began to press him to drop the "crazy idea".

Claire was far along in her third pregnancy as September ended. Bertie vaguely remembered Claire telling him it was an unplanned pregnancy. But at this point he paid little attention to her apart from her formal duties in the office. She came back to work quickly after little Max was born, with the three kids in tow. Once again Claire and Bertie worked together every day, and even on weekends when they met to keep packing research papers into labeled binders.

Bertie and Claire drew closer. For Bertie they were close enough for him to confide in her a recurring dream, a nightmare really, he had been afflicted with about an incident during the War. When he went silent, Claire wrote something on a note pad and gave it to him. She had written "Nighty-night, Bertie". He was amazed at its direct simplicity. Two nights later she sent him those words in a message. On reading the message he was overwhelmed with a feeling of peace and contentment, a sensation he had never before experienced. And to his surprise the dreams stopped. In the months to come she would send that message with increasing frequency. To him, it was extraordinary. He did not yet see the truth: he was falling in love with Claire.

Yellow Ribbons

He could see their faces, the faces of his men. He remembered the names, the names of the men he once led into combat. He even recalled some of the addresses in the States. Addresses where their parents or wives lived. These things came back to him at times like these, then as he busied himself with the task at hand, they faded out-back into the past, where they belonged. As a Veteran on Veterans Day, he had acceded to the request of one of his young patients, a seven-year-old boy named Sebastian, to accept an invitation to go to his school on this Day to be honored for his service. The kids would regale the assembled men in the school auditorium with voices in unison singing God Bless America and reciting the Pledge of Allegiance, joined by the invitees, who were all seated together on the stage. At the end of this marvelous demonstration, the children all stood, the Veterans leaving the stage and filing down the middle aisle applauded and cheered by the sea of students surrounding them.

Finally, those selected by the kids themselves fielded questions in each classroom. Bertie drew Sebastian's Third Grade. On the way over in his car before the ceremonies began, he was all nerves, worrying what these young kids would ask. Claire tried to buoy his spirits by sending him a message: "Aww, you will be fantastic". He knew he might have to dance around any query about the War itself. Just the week before, the now 10-year old Charlie had interviewed him as part of a homework assignment. The boy's last question asked what we're his best and worst experiences in the War. Bertie did some quick thinking and replied: "The worst one was getting off the plane there when we arrived. The best was boarding the plane 12 months later and getting out of there". The boy contemplated the answer for just a moment, then smiled broadly. Then they began laughing. The Third Graders' questions turned out to be benign, and he enjoyed himself enormously.

On the way back to the office, his mind again drifted back in time. He had remembered the Stateside addresses because of the letters he wrote to the parents or wives of the men he lost, those killed in action. Eleven men, eleven letters. He tried to personalize each letter, and he knew his men well enough to pull it off.

In his letters Bertie lied to them all- "He didn't die alone and didn't die in pain". After the War he went to see each family. Their gratefulness at these personal visits was heart-rending. They all wanted details about how their son died, and they all were so pleased just by Bertie's mentioning a few of the dead boy's qualities. The fathers invariably expressed their amazement that this "fine, upstanding Captain" had taken the time to visit them personally. Mothers were mostly silent and had a far-away look in their eyes. His Platoon Sergeant's wife turned out to be the hardest of all. The two of them, the Platoon Sergeant and Platoon Leader Bertie, had developed a close friendship. Both the same age, the Staff Sergeant and First Lieutenant began to think alike, and were soon on a first name basis, Mike and Bertie. Bertie drummed into his men an infectious confidence and competence and the men in turn gave the 24-year-old Lieutenant their absolute loyalty, as they came to see his tactical ability was second to none. He relied on Mike to be the key link to his other NCOs and the men, to make sure his orders were understood. Mike was not killed in action. He died on a California freeway the day after they arrived on the West Coast from Overseas. Back to the World, they called it. He had stopped at an accident scene. Crossing lanes on foot to help, he was hit by a car. No medals for that, Bertie thought. But wasn't it just like Mike, rushing to the aid of someone without a thought of the risks? The young woman had an infant daughter- he remembered Mike's pride in showing around the photo of the baby- going home at last to see his daughter for the first time.

The woman sat with Bertie and brought him some tea. He told her the baby looked a little like his father. She corrected him- she is the very image of him, she said emphatically. It was then he first noticed it. Neatly tied into her hair was a yellow ribbon in the form of a bow. In just about every town he passed through he had seen yellow bows tied to trees here and there. He knew what they were there for- only when the boys came home could they be taken down. Even with the War now over for six months, no one took them down. "I wonder when she's going to have the courage to take it off", he thought. The widow spoke to him in quiet tones and her lilting Southern accent had a calming effect on the young Marine Captain. They both mostly reminisced about her husband, smiling at each fond anecdote. After a decent time, he stood up. Time to be on my way, he said. He looked at the baby, a long look. Never got to see her, he thought. Then abruptly popped into his head phrases they always used, when somebody bought it over there or they were sent out again with no rest, : "There it is", "Sorry about that", "That's just the way it is", and if they had to get going, "Saddle 'em up, Sergeant, and move 'em out." He looked up and their eyes met, eyes now glistening with her tears. Without a word he hugged her, and he felt the tightness in her embrace, she is holding on to him as if imploring him not to go. He was the last link she would have to the last year of her husband's life. He pulled gently away from her, and, still in silence, turned and walked out. In the car, he looked back. She was standing at the screen door, and her face was obscured by the screen. But he saw one thing clearly:

The yellow ribbon.

Just One Look

"When you are old and grey and full of sleep,
And nodding by the fire, take down this book,
And slowly read, and dream of the soft look
Your eyes once had, and of their shadows deep;

How many loved your moments of glad grace,
And loved your beauty with love false or true;
But one man loved the pilgrim soul in you,
And loved the sorrows of your changing face.

And bending down beside the glowing bars
Murmur, a little sadly, how love fled
And paced the mountains overhead
And hid his face among a crowd of stars"- W.B. Yeats.

They sat but three feet apart, one cold and sunny late afternoon in January. They were just looking at each other in one continuous long moment. Neither looked away, fixing an intent gaze on one another.

Neither said so much as a word, or even blinked. Bertie had been kneeling on the floor with the two-month old baby, Max. Since the baby's birth he found himself unable to take his eyes off of him, only tearing himself away to see patients. When he arose and sat back in his chair, he noticed that Claire was looking at him, and it stunned him for a few seconds. But he recovered quickly and fixed his eyes on her. To Bertie, the look in Claire's eyes was unmistakable: an abrupt realization passed over her face, followed by an intense and unwavering stare; her eyes seemed to be burning and cutting into him. The look in her eyes was so intense it had the effect of transfixing him. The two of them sat motionless just looking at one another. It was as if she was gripped by an epiphany, and that, he knew, was exactly what it was: it was the look of love. She wanted him as much as he wanted her.

Claire and Bertie both now knew, and they knew it at the same instant- they saw at once that they belonged together. And Bertie immediately realized something else- he was a goner. If he had been teetering on the brink before that moment, he now fell for her all the way, and he fell hard. For him there was no turning back. In those few moments a fire was ignited inside of him for her that would never be extinguished. He saw in her eyes both love and desire. The room was cloaked in a dead silence. Bertie's shyness made him hesitate, but he was gathering the nerve to get up and go to her- then he started to rise.

Then came the startling, insistent ring of the telephone, shattering the spell they were both under. Claire was shaken out of her reverie, hesitated for a second or two, and then turned to answer it. Bertie's protest, imploring her not to answer it, came too late. He stood next to her, begging her to put off the caller. But now, thoroughly frightened by what had just passed between them, she ignored his pleas.

Had they come together that ringing phone might have been, in future years, a story they both would laugh about. But it was for him a hateful thing, a harbinger of a sad fate. They grew closer than ever after that day, but Claire would decide four months later to go back to the life she had always known, and they would remain apart.

She had inspired in him the poems he wrote for her; these amounted to songs in his heart, but the songs all died aborning. These two star-crossed people were separated. Perhaps she made the only decision she could make. It was, he thought later, almost as cruel for her as it had been for him. Later, he would tell her that her decision was as hard on her as it had been for him. She gave him that look, a look of recognition, that what he said was true.

She would try to bury any feelings for him and never allow them to surface again. But she would waver more than once, with happiness or heartbreak hanging in the balance.

Poems

(Poems written by Bertie for Claire)

Someday

Someday, when tomorrow for me never comes,
Think of me now and again,
And perhaps miss me just a little
As I miss you now.
Remember I have always kept you
In my heart, and that I have always
Prayed you would find a little corner
Of your heart for me.

And once in a while simply say:
"Dear Bertie,
Nighty-night."
I will hear your voice,
And smile.

Never Cease To Be

If only I could speak to you,
And give to you these Feelings you give to me,
Perhaps you will at last see
That which will never ever cease to be.

And yet I am silent, too shy
And afraid,
And let my chances fade
Away into the gathering end of each day.

So, will these songs of love
I long to sing to you see the final curtain?
Or is this only a sure and certain
Beginning of things to be?

Once not so long ago,
You gazed into my eyes
And I into yours and so,
There it was for us to see:

That which shall never cease to be.

Make Me Smile

If the night falls sad and dreary,
Then banish from my eyes so weary
The cares of the day.
Let me hear your voice and say:

I am here,
And I will sigh again,
And you will deny the night of fear.
Make me smile.

You have given me the gift of laughter,
You have stolen away my failing heart,
You have kept it safe ever after,
You shall always, as you have done from the start,
Make me smile.

Tell me now you will never leave,
Tell me now you love me still,
Tell me now that you forever will
Make me smile.

Hearts At Peace

I will remember them always,
You're saying to me "I am here",
Banishing all the fears
Drying all the tears.

Memory of it will come to me in all your "nighty night's"
And the calm that descends upon me,
The contentment and the stillness of a heart at peace,
Setting me adrift in a sea of Feelings.

Clearing a night of palisaded stars
Above me are your soft words coming to me
As if in a Benediction:
"Of course, I miss you".

Shall I not set your words to me
Out on the winds of time,
And crown them with eternal praise?
Gifts to me freely given.
Gifts that freed my heart at last.
Gifts forever cherished.

The longing within me grows:
Give to her a gift freely given,
Free her heart of all her cares,
Let her set sail on the Sea of Feelings,
Let me give you the still contentment of a heart at peace.

Dreams

I dreamt of glory,
I dreamt of fame,
I dreamt of riches,
I dreamt of love.

All glory is fleeting,
I am unknown,
Treasure is an illusion,
All these dreams have perished.

But one:
I dream of you.

Duty

(Soliloquy)

You will have a pain within
That shall never cease.
You will be plunged into despair,
That will be with you always.

Your every thought
Will be touched with sorrow,
A sorrow of emptiness
Devoid of Hope.

And because of these afflictions
You have accepted freely,
Many others will be spared them,
And will remain unharmed.

And no one will ever know
Of your Sacrifice.
And she will be gone,
Gone forever.

Thunderbolt

Up, up it climbed aimed
At the deep and clear and high sky.
His heart pounded as it gained the summit.
Then, the straight breathless downward plunge.
Thunderbolt!
At the Coney Island of his childhood.

Take the ride again, kid.
And when he grew up,
He would take that ride again.
And again....

Silence

The invisible ether is silent.
As if wandering in a dark forest
On the night of the new moon,
Only those like you, the lonely hearts,
Will know of your sorrow.

Enervating,
Deadening,
Embittering
Silence greets you.
Hope will not spring eternal in your breast.
Must these things be?

Will you drift on a retreating tide?
Without an anchor?
Not if she breaches the silence,
Not if she extends her hand,
Not if her voice comes to you
So sweet and strong.
Not if the nearness of her....

Are all these, once her gifts to you,
Have they fled and left you?
Drifting and broken, in the ether of....
Silence?

Tin Man

To simply harden the heart
Is futile, for it still will dwell in the breast.
To pretend it is not there, not vital
And warm, is foolhardy.

No, it must be cast out,
Discarded without thought
Or desire to find it ever again:
Only thus can you find
A certain Peace.

It will be neither a Peace
Of harmony,
Nor of love,
Nor of longing.
And what do you gain thereby?

You gain the false Peace of
Emptiness.
You gain the false promise of
Hollowness.

And you will lose the knowledge
Of that sure Truth:
That once you Love someone,
This becomes an eternal moment in Time
That can never be erased,
A bright beacon
That can never be extinguished.

And you will find your heart
Was always there, after all.

Somewhere In Time

Somewhere in time,
One sunny morn,
We will awaken to find each other again.
Somewhere it will not be too late for us.

Someday we will stroll together
On a quiet afternoon;
On a moon bright night
We will have our dance.

Somewhere in time,
In the light snowfall of Winter,
In a glimmering Spring,
In a shimmering Summer,
In an Autumn of vibrant color.

Where or when we cannot know,
Nor how we will find each other,
But it matters not.
For somewhere I will know your love,
And you, mine.

Somewhere in time.

Sins And Redemption

"Say you will share with me
One love, one lifetime.
That's all I ask of you"- adapted from Andrew Lloyd Weber, "All I Ask of You".

"My wife of 36 years, Carolina was the only woman or girl whoever said she loved me. Of the seven or eight girls before her only two were of importance to me.

Neither of them ever said that they loved me, and both showed me the door in different ways. And now Carolina has not told me that she loves me for many years perhaps 15 or 20. Despite my asking her to do so she has steadfastly refused with her silence.

My own part in this decline in our marriage does not do me credit. I have remained steadfastly loyal to Carolina for 36 years. I haven't fallen in love with anyone until recently, and apart from some harmless flirtations I have never ever made love in any way to any girl or woman. However, beginning in the mid-1990s I engaged in a different sin. This was the sin of Indifference. Both of us grew apart after 1995, both of us pursued our own ends. And it happened slowly at first but then from about eight years ago it began to accelerate. I bear the sole responsibility for the acceleration of this drift apart because of my indifference to my family. I told Carolina about a year and a half ago that this sin could never be forgiven, and I recognize that. Nevertheless, I had hoped to reconcile both of us by being the husband and father I had failed to be for a brief period in the mid to late 90s on through the early part of this century.

This turned out to be a forlorn hope. As I have pointed out elsewhere Carolina will not engage in public displays of emotion and this has now passed into the private realm.

I recognize that apart from the early years of our marriage this has always been true of her. Nevertheless, my failure to observe the obligations and responsibilities of a husband and father for those years has been the proximate cause of this decline."- Extract from Bertie's diary.

Yet he attempted a renewal of love. As the months passed with no response, despite his increasingly desperate pleas, he lost heart. She simply would not let him back in. He gave it up. And then he fell in love with Claire. Little did he know that just a few months later, Claire would cut him off as well.

So, he realized there would be no farewell when he left for New Guinea. Just here today and gone the next- not a trace left behind. He mused that of the two women that meant everything to him, neither gave him the time of day. With Carolina it would be, and had been, an abrupt turning of her back and off to something else, rather than listening to him. With Claire it was at times an impatience that almost said "get it over with" so she could pay attention to something else.

Thus, in any case, he was just about ready to give up on both.

During the summer and into the fall and early winter he tried vainly to romance his wife. Carolina hardly responded at all. She simply would not alter her behavior, moreover she had long before habitually spoken to him in a perfunctory and even a harsh tone of voice. Now, that harshness became constant. This had been preceded by a very difficult 18 months following a severe accident in which he suffered a traumatic brain injury. The subdural hematoma which resulted was short-lived. But the imbalance and mental confusion that followed was a trial for them both. Frustrated, Carolina increasingly began an otherwise inexplicable series of verbal denunciations. The personality changes and severe short-term memory loss induced by the injury were at first marked and slow to heal. In the event, memory loss extended to temporary, but frightening, total memory loss. At one-point Bertie even forgot who is own son was.

He recovered gradually, just a little "craziness" left in him, along with a serious short-term memory deficit. Summer came again, and on a lazy, hot day in July he came across a wedding day photograph of Carolina. Almost immediately he was once again struck by her beauty, then in a disconcerting rapidity fell into a grief-like state. Where had the years gone, he wondered. And even more cruelly-where had things gone wrong; what was it that really parted their anchor and cast them adrift, the countercurrents of their lives dragging them further and further apart? He had given up his hopeless attempt to rekindle their love. In truth, that love had fled her many years before. He had reasoned for a time that Carolina was just constitutionally incapable of an open display of emotion of any kind. It had not been so in the beginning. Perhaps there are but phases to a union of two people, united for life yet changing in much the same way that history's eras do - some theoretical "maturing" process. Nevertheless, such theories and turgid analysis had become inimical to him. His actions had always been guided by feelings, and never more than now. He ruminated on his life to that point. The journey to New Guinea lay only six months hence.

"I have had a good run", he thought, "first class education, Marine, survived a war, married a wonderful girl, we raised a fine son, made myself into a physician; wouldn't trade in this profession for any job in this world of ours. Met Claire and she restored me to the man I used to be. No regrets. Well perhaps just one: I will never again know the open love of a woman. But my heart is really at peace, thanks to Claire."- extract from Bertie's diary.

And Carolina? He loved her still. But it was apparent now it would be a silent love, perhaps even a fading one, devoid of much affection. And as to whether she had any love for him? She had refused to say. She took care of him, urging adequate sleep, sufficient nutrition, seeing his doctors regularly. Love in a way. Yet any other expression of affection was denied him. He had no choice but to accept Carolina's concept of what a marriage at their age consisted of. Even the most casual and small affectations of love were absent, and this condition was to be permanent. The barely suppressed fury she bottled up over the New Guinea expedition might in any case be that which would break them apart. Her diatribes were less frequent now, but the themes remained constant, the lectures themselves profane and almost vitriolic at times. It was after one of these explosions that he felt all was hopeless.

It was now clear, whatever sins he was guilty of, there would be no forgiveness. There would be no redemption from his real or imagined transgressions. At perhaps the nadir of their fortunes together she told him: "I do not want to remember you". Their social intercourse together would gradually improve, but open affection eluded them. Carolina simply would not open the door for him. Despite the most recent rescue of him from total despair by Claire- indeed she had renewed their relationship to a restored sense of comfort together- he now saw clearly that open love was closed off to him by both women. Even simple affection did not exist. So, as the days of the following summer reached their midpoint, his fear of a sterile life ahead loomed up quickly. Sterile, commonplace, cool and correct, all conventions observed- this barren future at first alarmed him, then to his great dismay, he saw he was being forced to acquiescence in what he regarded as a mere emotionless existence. And there was no way out. All roads to personal redemption and the rebirth of affection that he longed for dead-ended in a tangle of the protocols of conformity. And both women's emotional cachet was expended in other directions: Carolina's for her birth family and Claire's for her children. Since he regarded this as right and proper, he would not place his predicament at the feet of either woman.

Quizás

The Courtship of Carolina would consume two years. Bertie came to the Latin Island nation to study Medicine and play baseball on the side. Baseball would last all of two seasons, while Medicine merely scratched the surface of a life's work that would endure out to 35 years, and there would be more if Chance favored him in New Guinea, and he survived, for many more years.

They were never alone together during those two years; the formal courtship rules were maintained beneath a veneer of informality. Carolina's father had died when she was thirteen, and the respected Judge left behind a widow with her son Jacobo and two younger daughters, Carolina and Sofía Lissette. Carolina was just 20 years old, and Bertie was age 29 when they met.

Courtship consisted principally of many evenings sitting on the veranda, and simply conversing. The topics varied, usually something of local interest, but he soon fell into earnest discussion with her Mother- both of them shared a passion for politics, both national and international. Often, with Carolina absent, her mother and the future son-in-law sat alone and talked far into the night.

Carolina herself remained coy for the entire two years. Her constant refrain was quizas-perhaps.

The first two summers passed quickly, with Bertie playing baseball with some success, especially at the plate. He found the games exhilarating, regarding them as duels in the sun or under the lights, playing them with an almost violent exuberance, as if their opponents were the enemy.

The study of Medicine absorbed him- much of it new to him, and because of its newness he soaked it up enthusiastically, diligently, and by a method of constant repetition he mastered Anatomy Then Neuroanatomy. Having distinguished himself in the year end examinations he was named as an instructor in Neuroanatomy, teaching the next class of incoming students.

Baseball was now relegated to the past. Rote memorization of material was the method they taught- he cemented it in English, then translated it on paper for the examinations into Spanish. Then suddenly the formality of the classroom was behind him. In its place for the last year were rotations through the main specialties of primary care in the public general hospitals of the Capital City.

Here in these hospitals they would see their first patients. Public institutions like these were divided into 80-100 bed Wards. No privacy existed. In the Obstetrics wards women were giving birth on bare mattresses. In the one-story psychiatric hospital, the afflicted ones walked on the roof, talking to no one in particular. The students first case was a Tetanus victim: his face locked in a permanent grin- Risus Sardonicus, the sardonic smile. Only mechanical ventilation now could keep air in his lungs. His body periodically arched its back- Opisthetonos- his muscles poisoned by tetanus toxin. He had come in for an inguinal hernia surgery, and the story was dirty instruments had infected him. After four weeks he finally died. Another Code had been called, another cardiac arrest. This time his heart gave out entirely.

At the Neurosurgical Hospital a young boy, 10 years old, was carried in unconscious, having fallen off a bicycle and struck his head. Oblivious is a better word. His eyes were open, tracking side to side in a dance of nystagmus. Or the eyes would roll in their sockets (orbits), periodically. His arms were locked rigidly across his chest, and his legs were fully extended and fixed in extension, the knees would not bend. Thus, for the first time Bertie saw Decerebrate Posturing. The neurosurgical resident asked the mother to wait outside- the boy's skull must be trephined, a burr hole made in it, to relieve the pressure on the brain from swelling. Otherwise the brain, actually the medulla oblongata, or brain stem, would herniate and death would rapidly ensue.

In the O.R. a burr hole was dutifully drilled. Fluid under great pressure spurted out. But, perhaps given too much anesthesia the patient stopped breathing. Resuscitation did not last long. The resident called the code, hurried outside with an autopsy consent form for the mother to sign. She did so, then became wracked with grief, sobbing uncontrollably. Back in the O.R. The resident made a swift incision circling the boy's scalp, then peeled off the face down and forward. With a piece of skull neatly removed the complete herniation of the brain stem was apparent, wedged down into a Foramen too narrow to admit it. Skull and face were then replaced, and after the nurses cleaned up the dead boy, his mother was brought in. After a feeble attempt at comforting her, the students left her alone with her dead son.

"Amid all these events of my training, I will forever remember and cherish my time with Carolina. During the courtship she remained somewhat aloof from me, yet I knew this was but a part of a game, each of us having a specific role: Carolina the pursued holding herself just out of reach, but never too distant to discourage me completely, and me the pursuer full of ardor and inventing devices to capture her at last.

Her coy refrain as I pressed her for commitment was Quizas, loosely translated as Perhaps. When the contest was over and she agreed to marry me, her effervescence seemed to blossom fully. I will always recall and cherish the sheer radiance of happiness she affected, her joy at beginning our lives together. I was then fully devoted to her and remained so for the next 35 years. Our times of personal travail took a toll on our mutual loyalty, loyalty to our desire to stay together. Yet I still recalled with overweening emotions our dedication and the happiness we had as we took up the task of enduring my years of medical training and the wonderful years raising our son. Even as we entered the many months of crises after my accident, I regained an ardent longing to fall in love with her again. But it was to be for a long, excruciating time that she rebuffed my overtures at every turn, until I gave up on her almost entirely. Separation or divorce became a constant theme with her, driving me to despair."-Diary extract.

This stormy, downward spiraling roller coaster ride did not end with a sudden jolt. Rather it seemingly faded into a coexistence free of any serious clashes, but it was a detente of conformity to a staid and monastic life, one devoid of passion. Bertie continued to blossom and mature as a writer, but now his writings had no audience. Both Carolina and Claire eschewed any interest in his stories or poems. He reflected that he was now composing his literary efforts for no one. And so, he thought sadly, his written work might as well not exist. Indeed, with no one reading it, it took on an unreal aura, with no particular effect on anything or anyone, a useless exercise. Yet his hunger to write and his inspiration undiminished, he labored on.

Labor And Delivery

(After medical school Bertie is assigned to a Philadelphia hospital for his Residency)

The bone-tired OB/GYN Resident awoke with a start from his bed, a lounge table in L and D.

The moans of one patient in labor too long assaulted his frazzled brain. The damn Beeper was going off on the floor next to him. The ER wanted him right away. He was in the middle of a 57-hour marathon on call.

He bounded down 3 stairwells and burst into the blinding white lights of the Emergency Room. The ER Resident took him aside into an empty cubicle.

ER Res.: "There's a patient in six you gotta see."

So, they go into six.

There he sees the patient lying on the stomach, softly whimpering. It's a 40-year-old Male.

"Hey chief, this is a guy." He turns to leave, but the ER Resident catches him outside.

Forty-year-old male brought in with a porcelain Easter egg jammed into his rectum. "So what? Call Surgery, I gotta go do a C-Section."

"Well, we figured you could sort of deliver it with Forceps."

One hour later: one big Porcelain egg successfully delivered. Weight: 10 ounces.

Back upstairs in L and D, the OB Resident starts a vertical incision on the poor lady too long in labor. Nineteen hours to go.

Engagements

(An Essay written by Bertie on the Science and Art of Medicine, written during his last years as a physician)

Think of the profession of medicine is having two distinct faces. As physicians we characteristically adopt the first face, science, as our major contribution to the human condition. If you think about it for a moment, we fight constant battles on behalf of our patients. We are aware even in our subconscious that no matter how many battles we win we will lose the war. And yet we fight on. Why?

On the surface the answer to this question is there is no give up in physicians. You see it time and again: They just won't quit. Doctor of Medicine, all of them, dig in and fight the best of defensive battles, constantly reevaluate, modify, and sometimes scrap their tactical evolutions in the fight for a patient's life. Even simple illnesses are attacked with élan. Disease throws down the gauntlet. And a physician responds with every scientific trick that he knows, gives everything within him, to defeat disease. Theirs is a call to duty unique in the human experience.

And what of the second face? It is the most daunting quality a physician will be called upon to master. And master it he must. It instills confidence in our charges. It enables the patient to go forward and fight the constant skirmishes, engagements and battles against disease. Without it the patient will be lost before the first shot is fired. It has been enshrined as the art of medicine. It is nothing more than the ability and will of the individual physician to deal with people on a person-to-person level. To sit and converse with them; at the end of an interview to standup together, shake hands, and then come out fighting against the common enemy. Without the skill it requires, the doctor may have lost half the battle before it has even begun. He Must be willing and able to huddle with and calmly and decisively tell the patient what we are going to do together to win the battle. The outcome will more often than not turn on the physician's aplomb with this art. If you are then defeated?

Well then, the physician must remember this: It is not that you are defeated that counts, only how did you fight, and why?

Dreams And Last Salute

DREAMS

It mattered not to him how the dream began. Nor how it cascaded inexorably to it's

End. It always ended the same way: Frantically working to clear the jammed action of his rifle and forever failing to open it, to compel it to work. And there they were:

The enemy. Closing in on him relentlessly.

LAST SALUTE

The dream came again. And again. He was shaken. Though he sought comfort, there was none. No one to soothe his sweat soaked brow.

Thus, before he left for New Guinea he must go to the place where their names were inscribed: His men, his friends, departed so long ago. He now must say goodbye to them, to render them a last enduring salute. Perhaps to find peace; to bury forever the bitterness in his soul.

He wished her to be with him when he did this. For her to take his hand; to stand with him, to say to him: "It is not true that none, but the lonely heart can know your sadness."

They would hear, one last time, the plaintiff bugle call of Retreat. Then the soothing, restoring, trumpet notes of Tattoo. And at the last: the haunting melody of Taps:

Day is done,
Gone the sun.
From the lakes,
From the hills, from the sky,
All is well; safely rest,
God is nigh.
Fading light dims the sight,
And a star gems the sky,
From afar, drawing near
Falls the night.
Thanks, and praise for our days
Beneath the sun,
Beneath the stars,
Beneath the sky.
As we go, this we know:
God is nigh.

Goodbye, he whispered. Then he turned to her and asked: And I will see them at sundown, won't I?

Dakha

"War is a thief in the night. It steals from mankind the bright promise of youth"- James Reynolds Bertel

The Dreams had now taken on a frightening, sinister tone that tore at his very fabric. Failure to clear the action of his rifle with the enemy closing in upon him- this was now taken one step further, right to the point of inducing an overwhelming terror. An enemy soldier now caught him and thrust his bayonet to within inches of his chest. Awakening in time, but unsure if he was hurt or even still alive or where he was- he bolted upright in the bed and spun his now hyper- vigilant eyes over the bedroom.

So began his random analyses, over and over, of what he could have done differently at Dakha. He spun the web of the tactics again and again, remembering every detail, every tactical evolution, counting the mounting casualties in his tortured mind.

Only Claire could have delivered him from this hellish cycle. Maybe it was as simple as the power of suggestion, a placebo effect that worked every time. But the "Dear Bertie, Nighty-nights" were gone forever. His appeals to rescue him had seemed to have been directed at someone who could no longer hear them. So, he stopped trying and accepted the inevitability of the Dreams. The grand gesture, probably useless anyway, of a visit to the Memorial with her now was relegated to a forgotten idea- at least it was banished by her.

For the first time, he realized, she had made a promise she would never keep. And she had not, after all, meant what she said. "You cannot go alone" really meant he would not go at all. With all his pleas to her to help ease his pain, the pain of unrequited love, having been ignored, even ridiculed, he now no longer knew what to believe in.

Hold the enemy. Stop them long enough for the C-130s to evacuate the civilians from the last airfield available, these were the orders. Fight a defensive battle in place until signaled it was ok to get out. With an enemy force six times their size, those orders might as well have read "Fight and die in place". So, the Battalion was inserted athwart the single opening in the swamps that led straight to the airfield. The enemy was thrown back in confusion in their first attack, unsure of the size force of Marines opposing them. The enemy was bloodied, and they hesitated. Recovery was slow, slow enough for most of the Battalion to pull back and board choppers. Left behind was Raid Company as rearguard. With evacuations well along back at the airfield, the Company pulled out, even as the enemy began filtering around their flanks seeking a way through the devilish Mangrove Swamps. Now left behind as the only force left to stop or stall them was his Platoon. Sixty men, three already dead and five wounded. The Skipper gave Bertie the four extra machine guns and three mortars from Weapons Platoon as insurance.

It was going to be a near-run thing, he knew. They had to pull straight back through the only

Exit unhampered by swamp. And just as he gave the order to begin leap-frogging back, the enemy launched a second assault. They had to turn and fight. Bertie massed all seven of his machine guns facing the enemy. He told his men to throw almost everything they had left at them, and for a few minutes it worked. Long enough to now begin what had become a race for the exit, the enemy on his flanks desperately trying to cut them off. The Marines would be in a trap if the flanking forces got there first.

He lost the race by an eyelash, held up by the necessity of turning to fight the enemy closing up behind them. But to stay pinned down now meant they would all die in a kill zone. He turned to the platoon Sergeant and made one of those instantaneous decisions, the kind that you second-guess years later: they would face to the left and attack immediately into the flanking swamp and count on surprise to carry it off.

And so, they did; with the help of gaining immediate fire superiority they broke out of the Trap. The mortar men shot off every rocket they had left. Then the line of men, with the machine guns massed in the center, arose at Bertie's signal and charged forward straight into the enemy positions, firing as they charged. They broke over their foes and kept going right to the airfield. But the cost had been high: six more killed and 12 wounded. The Skipper and his radio operator were waiting with the last two choppers out of Dakha. The Lieutenant and the Captain were the last two to board. A moment later the enemy swarmed over the airfield.

Now he replayed it over and over again in his mind. Left, or right? What did it really matter?

He told himself you might as well have flipped a coin. Who would ever know if he could have saved more of his men if he had played it differently?

His obsessive analyses did no good. The Dreams kept coming.

Heart Of Darkness

"I knew more than anyone what faced me in New Guinea. And stuff just happens sometimes. There were a few dozen ways that things could go wrong in a hurry. If you roll the dice enough times snake eyes is probably going to come up. So, you better be ready; get your head in the game and keep it there. It was the same old stuff: don't hesitate, don't flinch if anything happened. You had to make an instantaneous decision and then aggressively carry it out if you ran into trouble. It was likely to be just like being in the war zone: long periods of monotony shattered by a few minutes of stark terror. I learned a long time ago there is no such thing as pure bravery. Courage should be defined as the will to put aside your fears for a moment and do a job. And fear would be ever present; what courage was not was an absence of fear.

Physically, everything I had in me would be put on trial. There were pestilential swamps and thick triple canopy jungle. There was nothing there akin to what we know as civilized life. Malaria was rampant, along with typhus, Dengue Fever, tropical ulcers, trench foot, parasitic infestations such as schistosomiasis and larva migrans, amoebic dysentery, Japanese Encephalitis, and a dozen other diseases that could get you.

The fauna was famous. Fruit bats slept by day, and they made a terrifying and abrupt racket is they flew en masse in the night. Saltwater crocodiles and sea snakes inhabited the Mangrove swamps. And we would have to wade through the swamps for a time. The sea snake was the most feared serpent. Its venom was 10 times more lethal than that of the cobra. It killed you quickly. There was no reprieve. Hundreds of pure white egrets flew about, then alighted on water buffalo. Giant 4-foot-long lizards stalked their prey in the thickets. Leeches lurked in the water and were perched in the canopy. Their sites of attachment to the flesh could leave you with non-healing tropical ulcers. The Death Adder lay in ambush along trail margins, hidden in the leaf clutter. I sent my brother a photo of the Adder- he wrote back "It's been nice knowing you"! The fetid, humid air was choked with malarial mosquitoes. October was the "dry" season- "only" eight inches of rain fell.

Nominally Christian, animism reigned among the tribes. The natives believed in good and bad spirits. Sorcery was widely practiced. More than one malevolent spirit inhabited the trees or swamps, waiting to drag you into the underworld. The natives believed demons lurked in the rain forests. One tribe fielded a so-called Witch Killer- he would plant skulls of dead witches along the trail leading to his village, as a warning to interloping sorcerers. Once in a while suspected witches were burned at the stake. Upon hearing this, Claire quipped as long as I didn't wear a dress and got my haircuts on time, I would be alright. She was always quick-witted that way. Once again, she had given me the gift of laughter. But, jokes aside, the native tribes, and my relations with them, will be the most dangerous part of my journey. This was brought home to me by a recent revelation: the truth about Michael Rockefeller's disappearance in 1962. He was thought to have drowned in a New Guinea River, but recently declassified Dutch files revealed he was actually killed by natives. One tribe near my planned area of operations, the Air Mati people, were practically an unknown quantity. Their name translates as "River of Death".

I began to have a nagging feeling that my number was up. But why worry? If so, there was nothing to be done about it. Just prepare as best you can, and then go there and do the job. I refined last letters to Carolina and Claire. I knew my wife would probably turn her back on me, as she threatened to do if I departed for New Guinea. I desperately wished for a last talk with Claire, to say goodbye, but also to tell her exactly how I felt about her; to talk things out. It occurred to me that she might not allow it. Her utter silence as to any expression of affection towards me left me with a dreaded feeling of futility. The walk in the park never developed. Even the expected in person support at the memorial vanished, and after that, I began to think she really did not care for me after all, and I was once again disheartened. She had in the past always pulled me out of this by being kind in some little ways and yanking me out of the hole I was in. I half- hoped she would not rescue me this time. Just stick to business I said to myself, and get used to it, better now than later. But the thought of not being able to see her one last time before I left in July was too much of a blow. If that happens, if I could not see her then, the burden of sorrow in me would be almost unbearable. I named New Guinea the Heart of Darkness, with a nod to Joseph Conrad's novel. Now I learned another heart of darkness had descended upon me, the kind that now began to do well in my soul."- Diary extract.

Fadeaway Kid

"Now I threw myself into preparations for departure. The first priority was to be physically fit: superior physical condition in fact. I commenced an exercise program of constant walking, push-ups, sit ups. At the urging of a good friend, Steve, I decided to look around for a personal trainer and engage in a gradually accelerating and structured effort to reach a peak condition that would be vital to take on the rough terrain of New Guinea."- extract from Bertie's Diary.

So, Bertie now finally resolved to go all out to get himself into top physical condition for the expedition. At least to get in the maximum shape for his age. He realized right away he was no longer the 24-year-old Marine Raider who cut his teeth in the jungles of Vietnam. He turned to a former Marine boxer and ex-police chief named Larry, who now made a living as a trainer. Larry was also an expert rock climber, and Bertie would tap this resource as well later on. As it turned out, Bertie had, by pure chance, found the perfect trainer - Larry, the former boxer. Because he was in effect scheduled for a heavyweight slugfest in New Guinea. Now, after all the research he had conducted, he knew that for three or four or even five weeks every day of it was going to be rough, and some of those days would be brutal. So, he asked Larry, once his core strength and power were in place, to train him as if for a big boxing match. Endurance would be emphasized, but to Larry the Core was that from which everything else flowed. Larry pushed Bertie relentlessly, taking him through every strength machine in the gym. He pushed Bertie right up to his limit in Dead Lifts, then the trainer pushed him beyond that limit. After initial boxing training, Larry introduced the ten-round simulated bout. Bertie was required to throw 100 punches per round, with a thirty second rest between rounds- a total of 1,000 punches per "fight". Bertie learned to dread Leg Days- he facetiously told Claire that when Larry said "okay, it's Leg Day, Marine", he wanted to run the other way. But it all payed off- towards the end, after 12 months of conditioning, Larry figured his strength and endurance had improved 200%.

"By now, my disposition was flat. I no longer smiled much. Claire seemed to distance herself from me and it affected me badly. I castigated myself for jeopardizing a good relationship. I turned to ratcheting up research into New Guinea- get your head where it belongs, I told myself, you are going to need everything you've got to avoid "meeting the magician" over there. My partner in the quest for Photo Queen, Paul, a lawyer from Chicago, had done prodigious research into the mystery of photo queen. We would be meeting at his home in Seaside Heights, New Jersey at the end of April to coordinate our research. I had already informed Paul that I was planning to go to New Guinea myself and just pursue the whole affair in person- get to the natives, they had the answers. Our objective was to find the remains of the 11-man crew, including my uncle, the radio operator, and his uncle, a gunner on the aircraft. We also wanted to find the wreck of the airplane itself, as we suspected it contained some remains. We wished nothing less than a formal burial for these men, missing now since 1944, in Arlington with full military honors. There was likely to be no communication with the outside world once I set foot in Northwest New Guinea. I would just fade away into the jungles and swamps, not to emerge for at least three weeks- if I emerged at all."- Diary excerpt.

Fate Is The Hunter

Now I gave up entirely. I was sick at heart. Her purposeful avoidance of me was now obvious, even to me. My writing flared up for one night, then died out. No more poems of despondency, and certainly none of my happiness. An attempt of indifference failed utterly. The burden of emptiness would now have to be borne alone.

New Guinea now demanded time in any case. The sobering truth of the ordeal that lay ahead had at last been driven into us. Now with a determination born of necessity, we began to plan against every one of the possible dangers. Secrecy was essential to our safety. We revealed our plans for the operation only to our associates, and then in a limited way.

The during a virtual ground level flyover of the VERKAM River I was shocked to see the truth changes of elevation, numerous rapids and fast, plunging cataracts. I now realized what we faced: the bows of canoes must be held parallel to the swift current, rudder amidships. Any deviation, slewing that craft off the centerline would result in capsizing. Besides drowning, the other danger was putting us at the mercy of the crocodiles and sea-snakes on the lower river. Moreover, the river was only navigable for twelve miles or so. After that we would be faced with frequent Carries through the surrounding mangrove swamps. Carrying places would have to be found, and sure-handed Coxswains must be selected. No signs of PHOTO QUEEN were seen on the satellite views, the banks were mostly choked by swamp-forest and secondary growth.

The use of the helicopter would obviate the numerous dangers, but I hesitated when this was brought up. Unless I could be used clandestinely, it would draw unwanted attention from the Indonesian overlords. I recommended a chopper be held in reserve for a possible dust-off or quick extraction. Strategy was simple: Avoidance; remain elusive, be unpredictable. We must maintain relative secrecy as to our possible moment, lest they lead us to false sites. With the Indonesian authorities my cover story as a World War II nut interested in artifacts, Wreaks and World War II sites had to be maintained and had to be convincing. Avoid he thugs who were sure to plot against us, avoid Indonesian Army patrols, avoid the guerillas – all these made the more difficult because we would be the only two tall white guys in the neighborhood, as Major Cushing liked to point out. Above all, when the time came, we had to engage the wholehearted help of the Native Tribes.

Gaining the truth of the Natives was a key objective, and it could also be a crucial point of the danger. If we walked into a village, we had to observe the natives closely. We knew if women, children, and dogs were absent, we were in for it, I would mean they regarded us a human prey, and it would be time to get out of town, as fast. Thus, in any number of ways Fate would stalk us. We had to be ready.

Officer And Gentleman

Much to Carolina's relief the Photo Queen-New Guinea operation had been postponed to May of the following year. The delay was forced upon him partly due to finances, but primarily because he had been told by his Trainer that he would be in no physical shape to undertake the grueling duel with swamp, jungle, and mountainous terrain that lay ahead, by September. Nevertheless, his physical conditioning program began rolling ahead relentlessly and would continue for eight solid months before departure. He knew he would be ready by May, then there would be no turning back. This new deadline served to enliven him in his struggle with the demands to conform. It provided the physical and mental drive to now concentrate on an attainable objective. And enable him to protect the two women who still meant all to him. And through his own faults and vices, he now reasoned, perhaps he had forfeited the privilege of receiving open affection from them. In Carolina's case he saw clearly that he was to a great extent the cause of great stressful triggers that plagued her. And despite her uncompromising state of mind, he was required by his sense of duty to lift her spirits when they flagged, and not to impose any undue worries upon her. Where Claire was concerned, he knew he had to cease imposing any overtly romantic overtures upon her, because it dismayed her. He knew this would test his self-discipline severely, but it had to be done. He simply knew that he could not be the cause of any distress to either of them. This was the path of an officer and gentleman.

As for his daily life, he resolved to continue to display his own affection in a muted form to both Carolina and Claire, and never to ask for any in return. He saw clearly that to a large extent they both led lives with which he had little to do, and the way to ease their paths through their own difficulties was to remove any pressure on them to do anything but pay attention to their first priorities. Selflessness after all was the hallmark of the gentleman he professed to be. So, imposition of a desire for affection would perforce be a selfish act. In this way he may have rationalized his own surrender to conformity, but it was after all the kind of correct behavior he had been raised to adopt.

So, his ardent pursuit of two women in succession settled into a sort of slow burn in the case of Claire and a benign neglect in that of Carolina. It was now an almost philosophical approach, the pouring of oil on a troubled sea, reducing waves of discord and dismay to mere wavelets. Suppression of his Romanticist nature began, a difficult undertaking at best.

To attempt to replace Romanticism he forged onward in mental and physical preparation for what would be the supreme test of his life, at least since the War. He affected a gentlemanly manner, but if one looked closely, that carriage of the urbane and courteous officer and gentleman was belied by what became a grim and hard determination to ready himself for whatever awaited him 15,000 miles to the West.

Burning Bridges

"Claire rescued me again the following week. All it took was her endearing way of calling me Ding Dong or soothing me with a Good Boy if I did something right. Or with one of her little phrases like Okie-Dokie. She warmed to me again, and all was right in the world for me. She made me smile again, briefly.

Moreover, the Kids were stellar. Charlie messaged me while away for the weekend. A bunch of emoji's one his iPad. He helped relieve a down in the dumps attitude. No communications at all from Claire, but Charlie came through. I was surprised and pleased. Three consecutive nights of terrible Dream had left me with little sleep. I knew it was silly, but Claire hadn't sent me a "Nighty-night" for weeks. Then back in the office the next week, Claire's daughter gave me a series of sticky notes, each with 10 hearts. Then she hugged me. She had me wrapped around her little finger. She began calling me Pop-Pop. I was floating on air. Max looked at me and smiled, laughed, and carried on an unintelligible conversation with me. By now I was paying close attention to his development. It was sheer bliss for me when I saw him.

But Claire remains very distant. Silent. I realized at last that I had made her very uncomfortable around me. So, it was all my doing, I had no one to blame but myself. And I had no excuse.

I wanted to explain to her that the pain and despair that enveloped me caused me to press her. But that was beside the point. I decided that if she wished to return to the way we were I would have to remain completely professional with her. It was time to accept the pain which envisioned in the poem DUTY. There would be no easing of that pain by her. Once again, I blamed myself for this. I just wanted to smile again and for our relationship to be the way it was. But because of my overzealous pursuit of her I had spoiled it. I did not intend any longer to bother her; no more romantic expressions, no more personable conversation beyond that which was necessary, I would go along with her preference for silence. Her messages had all but ceased; in fact, there were none any longer. And when they resumed, I know it would be all business. Messages from me would cease except for that required by my practice. Emails from me would no longer contain any flattering phrases and no more poems beyond the last three I had written, which, emotionally, I was compelled to give her, but that I would include in her weekly envelope. Although I preferred to read them to her I know she would not be receptive to the idea. I prayed that eight poems meant something to her, had affected her in some way some good way. But I knew that she would never tell me of this or admit it. The three last poems would be met with the silence which the first five were greeted with. Why she kept them I do not know. Nor does it really matter in the end. And I knew that the sorrowful emotions expressed in the poem RAIN would be my companions always. And all this would come to pass because of my stupidity. I would henceforth just have to take it and somehow go on.

And so, I would leave for New Guinea with nothing to come back to. My wife would turn her back on me; and Claire would probably no accept my plea for a last meeting. Carolina told me she would burn any last letter from me without reading it. As for

Claire she probably would be exasperated by it and I had no doubt she would throw it away. Although Claire would probably read the letter it would still be discarded; I hoped not but hopes have a way of disappearing. As for this journal, maybe curiosity would impel her to read it. I would ask to please read it in the hope she would understand how and why I felt so deeply about her.

This last blow to me, my last wish that Claire would take me and put me in her heart, something that meant everything to me, would most likely not be granted by her. It would be my way of knowing if she really cared a great deal for me. It would be something I needed more than anything, because it would ease the pain that would be my companion for the rest of my life. That was the only motive for it. But I still carried her in my heart, and this would have to be enough. It is just too bad, I said to myself again, that you cannot burn your memories as easily as you burn your bridges" – *Excerpt from Bertie's diary.*

Tin Man

HE ADOPTED. INDIFFERENCE ONCE AGAIN. JUST THE WAY HE HAD BEEN BEFORE HE KNEW HER. She had rescued him from it, from drowning in it. She had made him whole again, she had brought out the best in him, and she had restored him to the man he really was and had not been for years. And he was eternally grateful for it, more grateful than she could ever really know. Now she had thrown him back in, but he blamed only himself. The great and good gifts she had given him had been taken back; but once again he knew only, he bore the burden of guilt.

He no longer wanted to think about the things that had been taken from him. As a matter of course, thinking, analysis, emotion, had to be cast out from within him: the indifferent soul demanded it. But the emotional pain of his love for her could never be banished from whatever was left of his heart. That very love itself would stay with him always. The in different man could submerge these emotions for a time, yet they would always return, a chronic affliction that he had to accept. He now would be required, when these feelings surfaced, to suffer in silence, never to give them voice or let them escape. No one must ever know he still harbored an undying love for her. And his words from the poems DUTY and RAIN, whose afflictions he now accepted at last, would never be softened by her. He felt now he had misjudged her: and the very quality of mercy was indeed strained, it did not fall lightly, and she was not capable of giving the gift of Mercy, not to him anyway. He still had an abiding love for his work and his patients, but now the moment he had dreaded was upon him.

Maintain courtesy, kindness and helpfulness toward her- he really could never do otherwise, he could not inflict indifference upon her, in fact he was incapable of anything less than helping her without any hesitation whatsoever. It would the one expression of his affection he could not suppress. Her children he would always openly love. But his time with them was strictly limited by her; he was out of the grandfather business too.

However, his expressions of outright love for Claire would cease compliments, poems, writings, songs, escorting her to her car. And emails, banter, jokes, use of endearing names, florid messages, phone calls- these would all vanish. Strict adherence to business was all that would be left. She had also made clear first names should never be used, at least that's the way he interpreted it.

So, he thought, this bone-dry relationship, so contrary to his usual nature, appeared to be as cold as ice. Whether a natural and easy-going friendship could ever emerge again was beyond him. It would remain very distant until and if she decided otherwise. That's just way things turned out, he thought. Nothing new in my life, he said to himself.

He now set about burning his bridges behind him in earnest. There would no last togetherness to say goodbye, no expression of "Bon chance et Bon Voyage" would be forthcoming. He resolved to forget the plea to her about keeping him in her heart. And so, the Letter he had written her became a dead letter. He would never deliver it. It would remain in his desk drawer, along with his poems and stories. No one was interested in them anyway. He had transformed himself once again into a Tin Man. Hollowness and emptiness now replaced the desperate sorrow that had engulfed him now for two months. Renewal was a pipe dream. The end was finally here.

The Expedition and his work now his sole companions, he threw himself into a steady rhythm of toil. He knew being ready did not guarantee survival or success. You still gotta be lucky, he knew. But being lucky or not, that toss-up was out of his hands. Nothing could be done about it, so forget it, he told himself.

Serious planning for the search for Photo Queen now began in earnest. He resumed the organization of the New Guinea papers alone. He would not ask her to take up the task again. He was so afraid of exasperating her again, he now withdrew that burden from her.

In truth she had not taken it up for weeks. He thought of this as another hint to him, another tie between them she insisted on cutting. And finally came the denouement: she told him in the car on the way to work not to ask her for a ride to work again, she would refuse, she told him. He had gone with her each Saturday, viewing it as a chance to be with her and he genuinely had enjoyed her company and open conversation. Now that, too, was gone.

It occurred to him now that it was akin to a ruthless scorched earth policy. Nothing at all would remain.

It appeared now, and was confirmed in fact by her demeanor, that even her reminders to him were given in as few words as possible, and that this was purposeful, as was the total absence of his or her name from messages or emails.

So, their separation was finally complete. He could never have imagined it. Even with his resolve to now acquiesce, the extent of her antipathy shocked him.

So, he now gave up. It would be a silent surrender to a fait accompli. With her own silence in place already, his muteness was not even noticed. The void in him would never be filled.

With all now suppressed inside him, the Silence was a cross he had to bear.

And he would bear it alone.

Charity

"Let me live in my house by the side of the road-
It's here the race of men go by.
They are good, they are bad, they are weak, they are strong,
Wise, foolish- so am I;
Then why should I sit in the scorner's seat,
Or hurl the cynic's ban?
Let me live in my house by the side of the road
And be a friend to man."- Sam Walter Foss

All he wanted now was peace. Thoughts only filled with a generous and charitable spirit.

Like Homer's Hermit he wished only to live by the side of the road and be a friend to man. To have his thoughts unencumbered by strife. Cruel? Yes, once upon a time he had been capable of cruelty, but only physical cruelty in a war he wished only to forget. As for her, the time for sulking had long passed; now he only desired to ease her path. The waning hope that she would once again bestow upon him the gifts she had once freely given that Hope was now but a dimly flickering and distant candlelight, gasping and guttering vainly before it was extinguished forever. He reasoned that what she had done was not out of malice. Nor was it now still in place due to purposeful cruelty. Claire was not like that, he knew. Initially she had cut him off because, he was sure about this, she did not want to pour gasoline on the fire smoldering in him for her. He could not get through to her that that fire could never be smothered entirely; and it would dwell in his soul as long as he had life. Perhaps she still withheld her love simply because it had become an unconscious habit. And because she really did not know of the painful effect it had on him. If she could only truly understand, he thought, then she would rescue him from spiraling into the depths of despair.

Thinking in this vein gave him a measure of the tranquility he so desperately needed. His reasoning, whether truth or delusion, parried the thrust of bitterness that at times stabbed into his heart. The sense of loss plaguing him ran deeper than just missing the ways she had made him smile. The absence of that indefinable Feeling she had given him hurt him badly. Bitterness and its' enervating companion Indifference lurked just below the false veneer of calmness he tried to affect.

With the onerous weight of despondency that so often heaped itself upon him, he allowed pessimism to take over his spirit. Thoughts of "maybe my number is really up" in the context of the New Guinea expedition repetitively intruded into his psyche. And this he knew was unhealthy: it might lead him to take chances against his professional tactical judgment: he might act with a reckless abandon, and if his luck ran out, that would be it.

There were now times he figured he would welcome the lonely fastness of the rain forest-clad and uninhabited Foja Mountains. It was telling that he had already insisted on going into those mountains alone. This alone demonstrated more than any other thing just how far his fatalism had carried him. He now reveled in pushing Lady Luck to the brink.

In his mind, he had already been denied the happiness and peace he had desired so much.

Now fast approaching was what he viewed as a sure chance to demonstrate just how hard a man he could be.

In fact, it was nothing more than a desperate gamble.

Unexplored

"The lights begin to twinkle from the rocks;
The long day wanes; the slow moon climbs;
Come, my friends, 'tis not too late to seek a newer world.
Push off, and sitting well in order to smite
The sounding furrows; for my purpose holds
To sail beyond the sunset, and the baths
Of all the western stars, until I die."- Alfred Lord Tennyson.

As a boy he had read of and been captivated by the stories of the great English, French and Spanish explorers of North America. He committed their exploits to memory. In his mind's eye, and with his prodigious imagination fully engaged, he saw Champlain going up the St. Lawrence, Cartier shooting the rapids at Lachine near Mont Royale, Hudson sailing up the river that would bear his name. All the maps with their neatly drawn blue and red penciled lines of the explorers' journeys of discovery dwelled in his dreams. Now, grown to manhood and beginning the Autumn of his years, and just by pure chance, he stumbled across an unexplored range of mountains called the Fojas in New Guinea.

The Fojas lay just south of the operational area encompassing the search for Photo Queen. It suddenly occurred to him that it was marked unexplored on the maps and most all the Range had never been visited by so much as a single human being. Not even the nearby natives of the Kwerba Tribe had been up there. They contented themselves with abundant game to be hunted within an hour of their village. Ten days of hard marching, they estimated, would be needed to get up to a point near the fastness of the peaks.

And now it dawned upon him: if he ascended into the heart of the Fojas, he would be the first man, no, the first human being to explore the valleys, peaks, and ridges clad in pristine montane rain forest. As the first, he could claim the right of naming the peaks he reached, and he would draw the only maps in existence of those geographic features. He resolved to stay additional weeks if need be to accomplish his new mission. But this would of necessity come about only after he had exhausted all possible attempts to find Photo Queen and its Crew.

So, he turned to, taking up the planning of the Expedition, and his so far forlorn try at burying within him his burning desire to rekindle the natural ties to Claire he still longed for. And after nightfall, alone again on his veranda, he dreamed the dreams of an Explorer- dreams of a New World in the Foja Mountains, dreams of his own upcoming journey of discovery.

Destiny Or Fate

Which of the two was it to be? For they are not the same. Which or what awaits me on the other side of the world: he found himself pondering the answer to an age-old dilemma. Even with the busy preparations for departure, he failed to exorcise these questions from his mind.

For the Greeks the answer was an ordained fate, ordained by the gods. There was no escape from the clutches of fate. For the Romans the answer was an over-weaning belief in their destiny as a race. For the upstart Carthaginians it became both: their destiny rode with the armies of Hannibal, and then their fate as a race ended in oblivion. For the Arabs all they had to know of either was "It is Written", and for the Israelites their destiny as God's Chosen People was irrefutable. For the later Latin peoples "If God wishes it" was the watchword.

For him: was his destiny to find those men? Or would fate dictate failure? Did destiny dictate he would come back at all? Or was it his fate to die there? For all his pondering the answers were unknowable.

Bertie found himself, late into the night, sitting alone on the veranda, gazing almost vacantly at the clear star fields overhead. The answer to what awaited him in the Southwest Pacific eluded him with quick efficiency; nothing but the dead silence of the darkness was heard in response. "Which is it to be", he called out loud defiantly.

The distant and far star clusters remained as they had always been mockingly mute.

Then he suddenly thought of Claire. Did she likewise remain mute because to do otherwise, to acquiesce in listening to him giving voice to his poems directly and personally to her, would this betray her own emotions? She had always greeted his readings with obvious emotion or attempts to smother those emotions. Could that be the answer to her silence? Did she have feelings for him, after all? Feelings she would never allow to surface again. This epiphany, if that was what it was, was at once his answer as to both his Destiny and his Fate: he knew at once he must now find out which it would be. And there would be, there must be, he promised himself, a time and place for the answer. But she would have to grant him that time and that place. And then he could insist on an answer from her. But, perhaps, it was an answer that should forever remain unspoken. Bertie's thoughts swirled in a contradictory turmoil.

And, as for his Destiny or his Fate, he already knew that Chance alone would dictate which it would be.

Delirious Burning Blue

"Oh, I have slipped the surly bonds of earth,
And danced the skies on laughter silvered wings;
Sunward I've climbed and joined the tumbling mirth of sun-split clouds-
And done a hundred things You have not dreamed of:
Wheeled and soared and swung high in the sunlit silence.
Hovering there I've chased the shouting wind along
And flung my eager craft through footless halls of air.
Up, up the long delirious burning blue
I've topped the windswept heights with easy grace,
Where never a lark nor even eagle flew;
And while with silent, lifting mind I've trod
The high un trespassed sanctity of space,
Put out my hand and touched the face of God"-"High Flight" by John Magee, Jr.

Perhaps Bertie's finest moments in his relationship with Claire were associated with reading or reciting something to her. Whether it was a poem, his or others, or a story or lyrics to some song that struck his fancy, he derived immense pleasure from just sitting with her and imparting to her some literary piece he found beautiful. Or well-crafted, evoking very real imagery in him and, he hoped, in her. He drew a calming satisfaction from her unfailing attentiveness; she sat quietly and looked directly at him, patiently waiting for the latest offering.

And he was never disappointed, as, he quickly noticed, Claire responded in a manner that was unmistakably pure pleasure at what he had read to her. There were even audible sighs, as when he recited Jerome Kern's lyrics to "All the Things You Are" *followed by an eager rush of excitement as she leaned over to earnestly ask him where he got such a lovely verse.

Bertie smiled broadly at such moments, thrilled to the core that he could evoke such a demonstration of pure delight in her. With virtually everything he read to her he noticed the obvious joy or just simple enjoyment. He saw it in her eyes and her face, or perhaps by a little cry of a new discovery escaping her lips.

Looking back upon those, for them both he was certain, wonderfully satisfying moments, he recalled her excitement at listening to "High Flight" as though they both were, like the pilot in the poem, flinging themselves upward into the delirious burning blue "footless halls of air "somewhere above even the clouds. Bertie's Aviator father had read this to him as a young boy. He told Claire that it mirrored his father's pure sense of freedom while flying. Or her quiet approval of his poems "Someday "and "Dreams". Even her bursts of nervous laughter on the occasion of two more of his poems struck a chord of happiness in him. For the laughter was intended, he saw at last, to conceal some emotion welling up in her. And so, he laughed right along with her- she always had had an infectious effect upon him.

And she had accepted a packet of copies of his poems with genuine thanks, and, he saw, a very real, almost girlish, joy at knowing they were written for her alone. Thus, his stupidly over-sensitive despondency, triggered by his perception that she had ignored the poems, was revealed to be just a lot of fluff, "Much ado about nothing". In fact, they probably affected her too much.

To his great sorrow, the readings faded out. And they vanished for reasons he was well aware of: they had become too endearing for her to continue, and they disappeared along with everything else when she cut him off for those terrible two months in the spring. Bertie longed to restore the Readings. It seemed a damn shame, he thought, to ban those moments of delight and joy, something that brought a few moments of escape to them both. But the wonderful words rang out no more, replaced by an empty dead silence. The "surly bonds of earth" now held them fast. No more would an emotional piece of writing launch them into the burning blue.

It had become one of those voids in his life, and he suspected in hers as well, that invoked a certain sterility in their relations with each other. She had already restored much to him. To fill that void would be to restore a blessing for them both. To allow an emptiness to reside there would allow that blessing to die.

* "You are the promised kiss of springtime
That makes the lonely winter seem long.
You are the breathless hush of evening
That trembles on the brink of a lovely song.
You are the angel glow that lights a star.
And all the dearest things I know are what you are."- Jerome Kern.

Sound And Fury

He stood by the office door, because she had told him to remain there: Twice on her way out- in that brisk, hurried manner that she affected. Every time they said goodbye, she duplicated her exit: quick-marching without so much as a glance at him until safely ensconced behind the wheel of her car- then she put the window down, looked directly at him, and said see you tomorrow. She quickly drove off, but almost invariably gave him a few waves of farewell.

On this occasion Bertie stood looking at the ground in stunned silence. He was angry with himself for even the attempt to read her two poems she had clearly loved in the past. Claire's reactions to them were unprecedented. And those reactions had just shaken his faith in Claire. She had just taken him into her heart, just as he kept her in his, only a few weeks before. He thought to himself: she actually did stand up in the middle of my recitation and turned her back to me. Bertie was so surprised by this both figurative and literal volte-face, he was helpless to do anything but try to continue reading, but he had lost the heart to carry on.

Claire pretended to be looking intently at the photographs on his shelves. Her face was hidden from him. She spun about after one of his stammering objections and said she did not like being read to. She then went from one reason to the next rapidly and seemingly emphatically with no pause. What she had done was, in effect, to deny that she ever was enamored of the readings.

She not only gave lie to the poem he was reading; she had all but said the entire poem was his delusion. Bertie's emotions floundered about; he was incapable of making sense out of what had just happened.

Later, he was lost in thought, trying to make sense of what had transpired. There were only two possible explanations, he thought. One was simple and obvious- she really did abhor the times they spent together as he spun out some piece of writing.

This cannot possibly be the answer, he declared to himself. The wholly genuine excitement and pleasure she derived at such times might as well have been written in stone. He was not delusional with regard to that. Yet it distressed him overwhelmingly that he could do nothing right in her presence. Things always seemed of late to degenerate into an abrupt ending. And, of course, he knew why. It was his insistence on romanticizing something or other- which Claire, for whatever reason, was now refusing to listen to.

The only reasoning that made any sense at all was she had engaged in a flurry of mostly feigned impatience to deny any emotional display on her part. It was easier to do this because she wanted to get to a gathering of friends in her home. But it was not, it could not be the sole motivation for what he had just witnessed: impatience carried to the point of rudeness. This was not the Claire he knew. She was simply incapable of such behavior- it must have been triggered by her hearing once more the two poems that had excited and pleased her in the past. Impatient? Yes, he thought. She really had wanted above all to just get home. But rude and crass, denying any delight in the past? Saying to him in effect, that his poem was pure illusion? That was surely contrived.

Perhaps she just did not want to revisit the emotions and, yes, even the sincere feelings she had once had- feelings that came very close to love. Or perhaps he had been completely wrong. Maybe even her pledge to put him in her heart was just an expedient to rid herself of a pest. Although he dismissed that idea as impossible, it was eating its way into his consciousness. He was thinking too much again. Claire would probably dismiss him with "don't get your panties all in a bunch". Yet there certainly was no attempt on her part to ameliorate the insult to his pride.

So, his carefully considered withdrawal to a benign and easygoing gentlemanly world had failed its first test. Thus, Bertie's anger with himself. There was nothing to be done to recoup the lost ground. He must now just pull back without a sound. The next day he would, in a formal manner so unlike him, apologize to her, accepting responsibility for what had occurred. He even informed her he would not trouble her again with any writings, knowing how hard that would be for him. These were the obligations of an officer and gentleman. He had distressed her, and that was unforgivable in his mind. Thus, his retreat, and acceptance of defeat would be final. Life itself was, indeed, Bertie now recognized, as Shakespeare had divined long ago:

".... a poor player, who struts and frets his hour upon the stage, then is heard no more. It is a tale told by an idiot, full of Sound and Fury, signifying nothing".

His writings had, in effect, become not just unsung, but must be ignored and unmentioned. Any demonstration of affection, no matter how small, became a dead letter.

Indeed, the opposite had just happened- dislike, dismissal of something he held dear. For heaven's sake, he thought sadly again, Claire even turned her back to me.

To see him then, one could only describe him as stricken with grief.

When he turned out the light that night, sleep would not come to him.

When it finally arrived, it was a benediction to a man who had lost heart.

Running On Empty

Dear Claire,

What I mean by giving up is it is time to carry out the pledge I made in the poem DUTY. And to do it completely: to end my hopeless quest to win your love, as hard as that will be on me. I have tried, believe me, to do this time and again, and found my effort to be useless. I loved you too much to give up. But I now guess I am what I was called months ago- an old fool. But maybe if you consider that everything I did or said or wrote for you was because of love, you will judge me less harshly. As for me, I must just forget about it. I've got to leave you alone and no longer impose burdens on you. My feelings are genuine, but not overtly returned in kind, and that is just the way it is.

I realize now that what you said of me is true- I am annoying. I can only hope you will not remember me that way. I wrote in my letter to you to remember me instead as a man who would have devoted himself to you, and a man who would love you to the end of his life. Any of the seemingly crazy, childish, or silly behaviors

I exhibited were those of a man desperately in love, and seeing things slipping away. Because you have never confided in me or told me otherwise, I must take you at face value. So, as much as I thought or wanted to believe that you once, and perhaps even now, had feelings for me- was this but an illusion? Yet I know I was not wrong about the way we looked at each other that day- it is burned into my memory: no woman had ever looked at me like that before. Although I had fallen in love with you the month before, it was those precious moments that sealed it for me- after that, for me, there was no turning back. Ever since then, my love for you has run deep. We both knew in that single moment that we were looking at the person we were meant for. But by some cruel twist of fate, it never happened. And now it is too late.

But now, what difference does it really make? None. I could never accept that it was too late for us. But so, what? My stubborn refusal to accept defeat makes no difference at all.

Now all those pathetically little things that gave me some measure of happiness must be jettisoned. And I will never know for sure if seeing me at any time or other brightened your day. You have never told me it was so. I just saw that in your face. Maybe these times were also my illusions: walking with you to your car, sitting together in the office and enjoying each other's company, sitting at a table putting together papers and files, sitting together whilst I read to you some poem or story(some of which you loved), riding in your car together and just talking, and your wonderful messages- both of us smiling and laughing over your "insults" and names you gave me, your "Dear Bertie", all the Nighty-nights; my invariable compliments to you on your beauty every time we saw each other. I cherished all of the little time I had with you and all these will vanish. It will be as if they never existed. We will go on leading our separate lives, and if all you want is just a formal, sterile, and cold relationship, then that is how it will be- there is nothing I can do or say that will change that. It seems I cannot cheat despair; it will win, and a terrible emptiness is all that remains.

All that is left to me now, all that I will ever have of you, is your promise to keep me in your heart always. To me, that itself is Love. I put you in my heart long ago. To me, it means that in some sentimental way we will always be together, after all. And I bless you for it because it will ease the pain of not being with you. I loved you and I will remain in love with you, and it is not wrong to love you. If you still harbor any love for me that is not wrong. My only regret is that you never told me it was so.

Love,
Bertie.

Daybreak

"Someone might ask why it is important to me to be with you at any time or other. Whether running errands or just sitting together somewhere, alone, just the two of us.

If you are here and I am here, and no one else, then I may be allowed my illusions. And it makes me smile. Someone might ask: What difference does it make? The answer is sadly None. Unless you smile too. Then it makes all the difference in the world. And daybreak will come to us both. If not, then the illusion must suffice, and as in a false dawn the light will be extinguished again when you leave me.

It occurs to me now I have been waiting for the sun to peek over the Eastern horizon forever, and forever more I will continue waiting. Hold on through the night, hold on. Even though there is nothing there in the darkness to lean on, one must have faith.

For someday you may emerge from the night and bring the sunshine with you. Only this time you will not leave me.

I will look up, squinting into the sudden light and, seeing you, I will smile again. And you will smile too.

Daybreak.

Daybreak, at last."- extract from a letter from Bertie to Claire.

Finish Line

It was a crisp evening in the early fall, late September; he was sitting again on the veranda alone. Bertie mused to himself, that he was akin to one of those lonely long-distance runners. Having toughed out a grueling year of working towards the finish line, he suddenly found himself back in the starters' blocks.

Operation Photo Queen had been put on hold until the following spring. This, in and of itself, was enough disappointment for one year, of planning, researching, and painstaking study of the terrain, native cultures, the flora and fauna (especially the dangerous kinds) of New Guinea. The Expedition was the Constant factor in his life now, however. And come what may he would depart in the spring.

What stuck in his throat and pained him without mercy was the regression of Carolina to her inflexible ways, and the continued stand-off between himself and Claire. The entire year had passed in fits and starts- retreating 100 yards for every 101 yards he advanced. And it was mostly, he figured, his own doing. Another self-torturing weekend was upon him as he sat in the chill autumn night. Another weekend without seeing Claire, and another of Carolina pushing him away.

Frustrated beyond words, Bertie cemented a determination in his mind to lay out everything in the clear with Claire. He simply could no longer keep it buried inside him. He had tried time and again to give up, but it had always been futile. The inexorable clock was running out on him, at least that relentless analogy kept on eating at him. He now at last was impelled to earnestly and tenderly lay his case before Claire. He must tell her he loved her. Springtime seemed distant now, but in the blink of an eye, he feared, it would be here- and he would be gone, with all the stinging regrets of inaction and irreplaceable Time lost forever. And who could say with certainty for how long? Would it even matter to her if perchance they were fated to never see each other again- with time, surely all traces of remembrance of him in her would fade away and be erased. These fears plagued him, though he told himself they were irrational. But the great fear that weighed upon him was what would happen when he bared his soul to Claire. Yet Bertie knew he could not withstand another six months of leaving the outcome of his love for her twisting in the wind. To go on loving her from afar, as it were, was not in his nature.

So, the lonely distance runner would now sprint abruptly for the finish line. Fulfillment or sheer heartbreak waited for him at the line.

Which one it would be mattered little to him now.

That last chance glorious charge, so ingrained in him, was all he had left to give.

All Dear Names

"I have been so great a lover: filled my days
So proudly with the splendour of Love's praise,
The pain, the calm, the astonishment,
Desire illimitable, and still content,
And all dear names men use to cheat despair,
For the perplexed and viewless streams that bear
Our hearts at random down the dark of life......

And to keep loyalties young, I'll write those names
Golden forever, eagles, crying flames,
And set them as a banner, that men may know,
To dare the generations, burn, and blow
Out on the wind of Time, shining and streaming...."- from "The
Great Lover" by Rupert Brooke.

Ever since Bertie got the stuffing kicked out of him by Claire the day,
he attempted to read to her an old poem he had rediscovered, he was
caught up in a cycle of despondency, sentimentalism, and a nagging

feeling that he had lost faith in her. Then he realized that none of that mattered after all, if he had misjudged her, or if he had placed too much of a burden upon her. So, he finally struggled to adopt a bearing of ambivalence. He decided that the whole affair, concocted by him, pushed by him, had been a failure. He had been a failure. He now told himself he was tired of thinking too much. All he knew for certain was that he had loved her without any reservation, that he remained in love with her, and that he would never stop loving her. But this had become an exercise in futility. He now knew he had to give up for good. He mused that he felt like Lee must have felt at Appomattox: utterly defeated, and there was nothing left to do but go and see Grant. And, as at that fateful meeting, all of the sound and fury would be overcome by a stillness, an end to speculation, an end to theories and analysis of his or her motives at any one time or another. An end to any pressure whatsoever upon her. After all she was just a human being, put on the spot by him any number of times, and did it really make any difference if she had loved him for a few moments or days or weeks? The answer to that was yes, for him, but not at all for her. She was able to shed any thought that they belonged together, because she had a life to go back to, no matter the doubts she may have once harbored. He only hoped that she knew that everything he had done or said or written to her had been due to love. Perhaps if she knew this, she would judge or treat him less harshly.

Bertie, on the other hand, had nothing much to turn back upon. The same romance-less life awaited him. There was no place to "move on" to. To become the Indifferent Man, the Tin Man, once again was at once inevitable and unavoidable. It had been his habitual character for years and would be so again. No woman, in any case, could ever live up to his label of "perfect". He now castigated himself for his so-called misjudgment. For he had not been wrong about her-he had misjudged himself. He would not put any blame on Claire for any real or imagined frailties she may have had.

Whether or not Claire ever truly became his close friend was irrelevant. Bertie would have to shed his idealistic bent for some sort of "happy ending" and simply allow things to take their natural course. He could curse the Gods or his lack of luck with women. He would swallow this bitter draught- just when he found the One, the woman who fit him perfectly, it came too late. Half a lifetime separated them. Although he knew he would have given everything inside him to her for the years left to him, it made no difference whatsoever. That, he tried to convince himself, was just the way it turned out. Thinking about it from here to eternity would not change anything.

So, he just gave it up, stayed back in his office when she was there, remained unfailingly helpful and courteous, attended to the children as much as he could, and did nothing at all that would reveal his unquenchable love for Claire. It would be a love he would carry with him to the end. All he had left was the blessing she had given to him- that of keeping him in her heart. And keeping him there always. The utter selflessness of this single act would allow Bertie to cheat despair. And maybe this single blessing she gave him: wasn't that also called Love?

Time

"Ah, Love, let us be true
To one another! For the world which seems
To lie before us like a land of dreams,
So various, so beautiful, so new,
Hath really neither joy, nor love, nor light,
Nor certitude, nor peace, nor help for pain.

And we are here as on a darkling plain,
Swept by confused alarms of struggle and flight,
Where ignorant Armies clash by night. - from "Dover Beach" by
Matthew Arnold.

"When spring breaks through again next year, I will be gone. Who
knows if we shall ever meet again?
    I am tired of analyzing, theorizing, speculating. Tired of
thinking. I know only one thing: I have loved you, I love you still,
I will love you until I have no life left in me. I want you to be the
last person I see before I fall asleep and the first person that greets

me when I awaken. I want to share everything with you. I want to hold you and never let you go. I don't know any plainer way to say it.

I have never seen a woman look at me the way you did that day. Your eyes were burning holes in me. We both knew in that instant we belong together; words were not needed. It was as if we were joined and bonded together – looking into each other's eyes and knowing that we were looking at the One we were meant for, our One and Only. Moments like that are rare. Those moments are a gift to two people. It is given to very few people to find each other this way. We must not throw it away.

Every time we are together, I have this awful sense of what is missing. We talk, we smile, we laugh, we comfort each other in bad times with our understanding and genuine words. But the other half is just not there. That laughter, those comforting words, these do not end as they should in us holding each other, either smiling or crying, but these moments end with us apart. At such times I have a sense of loss, of emptiness where there must be human warmth and the healing touch of each other.

I have tried to give this up. It should be easy, should it not, for me to just turn my back on you and walk away. And then descend into ambivalence and indifference tinged with bitterness. The thought of going back to the days when I knew only these scars on my life is almost unbearable. Once, you rescued me from them.

Time is running out on us; we mustn't wait for things to be right, for the right time and place, because it will never come. The time is now, and the place is where we stand right now. I can't accept that "it's too late". We have been granted time together; we don't know how much time we have, but we've got to take it now, to make it count for something. It may be all we will ever have together. If we don't, then there's nothing more to it than to go on with our separate lives. And there will be nothing to remember. Whatever memories there are will fade and die.

And this too I know you put me in your heart, to keep me there always. God knows I put you in my heart long ago. That's called love. Love me, Claire. Love me.

And let me love you."- Letter from Bertie to Claire.

All Her Tomorrows

It wasn't until after that awful evening that the illusion took hold. Bertie's declaration of love was met with a burst of laughter that shocked him. It was for her a laughter of frustration, Claire told him later when he asked her why. She had urged him once before to stop it, to stop torturing himself, to end the hopeless quest to bring them together. She had long before this buried her own feelings and would not let them out again. His apparently mistaken belief that it was a nervous laugh to cover up her own love for him was exposed as a figment of his fertile imagination. Or so he thought. Later, he could not give up the sense that that laugh was really a cover for her real feelings. Her ultimatum that followed of leaving for good if he persisted crushed him. To him the look in her eyes that day long ago was unmistakable: she had realized she loved him. But this fateful evening found her love sealed within her. She had resolved to never allow it to surface again. And she did this for three good reasons- her three children must not be hurt. In this he stood with her. Any abrupt change in their young lives would hurt them- they simply would never understand it. But it hurt him that she would not allow him to talk it out with her. Instead she broke his heart quickly. Then shattered it. She never really understood that his love for her would never end, he would carry it with him to the end of his life, and thus the torture would never end. Moreover, she gave him no chance to implore her to see that they could have time together, however brief, to love each other before that time ran out and he left for New Guinea.

The new illusion was a way for him to temporarily deflect the great pain that now beset him.

He would reflect on what a grand life it would have been- for him a life-long love affair, an unswerving devotion to her. He would have shared every twist and turn that life offered without blinking. And she would stay by his side and pledge to him all her tomorrows; and an easy grace together, coupled with a life-long burn of passion, would ensue. It mattered not to him that once he returned to bitter reality the pain would be all the greater- he had no choice but to bear it anyway. And from that time forward he must maintain a Sang-Froid, a ruthless outward self-denial to show any feelings whatsoever. Lest he be accused of "pouting" when the truth was, he was filled with sorrow.

A persistent recurrent dream beset him. He was trying to reach her, to be by her side, to embrace her- but he could not- only a few feet separated them, but it might as well have been a mile. And it was as if she did not want to be reached. The change in their fortunes was demonstrated by a dream that came to him after that day in which they had locked eyes with one another: he was trying to reach her, and this time she took him by the hand, and they held each other. And then he asked her to give him her tomorrows.

But now all those tomorrows were only the bits and pieces of a broken hope. In six months, Bertie would be gone- the sooner the better, he now said to himself. When, or if, he would come back was still a mystery.

Whatever Claire thought of that, if anything, she kept her own counsel.

As with so many other things when it came to Bertie, she was silent.

Home Is The Sailor

"Here he lies where he longed to be,
Home is the Hunter, home from the hill,
And the sailor, Home from the sea."-adapted from Requiem, by
Robert Louis Stevenson.

"In only a few months' time my son will have departed to somewhere
across the vast Pacific. I will miss him each day that goes by; and I
will, like countless other fathers, silently tick off the days that remain
of my lonely vigil. I have never had such pride in him as I have now.
And I have never had such fears for him as I do now.

I remember now, as I write these words, the sheer happiness and
excitement that enveloped me the frosty morn he entered this world.
I remember:

The fearful moment I let go of him taking his first steps and
seeing his face twisted in anxiety, then that same countenance
laughing and smiling with pride and relief as he succeeded.

The evening he said to me "Daddy, watch me read", then smoothly and with a sure cadence read to me for the first time "Marvin K. Mooney Won't You Please Come Home".

Him standing in his crib with the brightest smile I have ever seen, welcoming us into his room with excited laughter one morning, his bright blue eyes sparkling with love for us.

Watching Carolina lying on her back balancing his giggling form with her arms and legs, tossing him into the air and catching him deftly as he squealed with delight. I sat watching this, not able to speak, just saying to myself: this is where I belong.

Fearfully letting go of the handlebars and watching with bated breath as he began his virgin run on his little bicycle.

Sitting in the pews each and every Sunday with him fidgeting between us at Mass.

His earnest question to me at an amusement park one sunny afternoon: "Daddy, can we live here?"

His eager agreement with me the day he caught his first fish. I told him "Jimmy, let's get this poor little sunfish off the hook and put him back in the pond". I let him toss the sunfish back in and noticed his immediate relief as it swam away quickly. Jimmy looked up at me and exclaimed "He's happy, Dad".

Crying with him in the torment of the grievous mistakes he committed in his adolescent years. And knowing I alone bore the responsibility for his failings. And telling him Tomorrow is another day, son. Things have a way of turning out after all.

Us just walking in the park on a brilliant afternoon one spring day, his tiny hand clinging to my index finger. He asked me quite suddenly: "Daddy, why do you Never Know?"

That day he came home, solemnly saluted me, and told me of his oath he took that very day to enter the United States Navy. Later, I almost wept with pride, knowing that when his country called, he stood up and answered the call, when so many of his peers remained seated.

And now my little boy is a young man. He struggled to find his place in the world. And he will struggle again. For now, he has purpose, he has found his sense of humanity. He said to me quite sincerely, "I love what I am doing because it is our pledge not only to defend our country, but to do good in the world, to help all people to enjoy a better life". With this I knew my son had found Honor and Duty. He had grown into the man I had always wanted him to be, not because he was wealthy or famous, but because he now understood what it was to be a decent man. And I remembered that long ago, wrenching day when my father, saying farewell unto me, as I embarked on my journey into harm's way, said of his hopes for me:

"No matter where events take you, son, just remember, always be a decent man".

After my Boy has gone to sea, I think I may once in a while go down to the water's edge somewhere along some coastline, look out to the horizon, and I'll imagine him at his ship's rail, perhaps on Watch. He may be gazing out to the horizon, too. Somehow those moments will bring me closer to him. Yes, it is but an illusion of mine. But it is all I have, until the day he comes back to me.

Until the sailor is home from the sea." (From Bertie's Diary).

Home Is The Hunter

"Under the wide and starry sky
Dig the grave and let me lie.
Glad did I live and gladly die,
And I laid me down with a will.

This be the verse you grave for me:
Here he lies where he longed to be,
Home is the sailor, home from the sea,
And the hunter home from the hill."- Requiem, by Robert Louis
Stevenson

It was quite sudden when the feeling came over him- rather it invaded
him without any warning. It was more a terrible realization than any
feeling. He knew almost immediately why: it gripped him with the
abrupt truth that he would never know Claire's love. It degenerated
into a hollowness in the pit of his stomach; an emptiness. It was more
than that. All hope had been taken from him.

The man who never quit was being forced to give up. The man who never knew the grief of total defeat was being compelled by force-majeure into unconditional surrender. The man who would never say die was dying inside himself. His fondest dream suddenly gone, an utter hopelessness was all that remained.

He had stopped his car in the gymnasium parking lot, and sat in it for a long time, stunned by what had just happened to him. Trying to reason it out, it occurred to him that he was being compelled to adopt the afflictions of DUTY- the decision to do so taken out of his hands. It was ironic that he himself had written the bleak words of DUTY, dictating a brutal emotional fate. His struggles within himself to subject himself to those words, his interminable delays, meant that she must decide for him. And that is precisely what she did. He had knowingly designed the ultimate outcome. But she imposed it. Maybe the way she did it was inevitable, but he was still bitter- if she only had allowed him to talk it out with her. He was saved from further torment only by his physical training session.

Bertie tried to shrug it off, but the thoughts of its implications stayed with him. But he resolved not to bother Claire with it. He would never put her on the spot again.

And he was painfully aware that the inexorable clock was running out the string. Ironically, he and his son would both be departing at almost the same time, both bound west to cross the Pacific- Bertie would be slogging through the jungles of New Guinea, which lay in the Southwest Pacific. His boy would be at sea, somewhere off to the North, in the Western Pacific. It was Jimmy's first Great Adventure. Bertie's thoughts strayed to his own first, which, forty some years ago, landed him in Indochina- only 700 nautical miles to the Northwest from the New Guinea coast. The geographic ironies struck him again and again.

Just another 700 nm. Northwest of Vietnam was the airfield in India from which his father flew into China in 1944. At that same time Bertie's Uncle Jim, his mother's brother, was flying in a B-24 named Photo Queen from his base at Biak Island, just off the

Dutch New Guinea shoreline, on the mission from which he never returned. And now, 70 years later, Bertie would be searching in New Guinea for the wreck of the Photo Queen and his uncle's remains. Who knew where his boy's task force would take him? Indian Ocean off Afghanistan? Persian Gulf? Perhaps they would patrol off the China Coast. Or even the Southern Philippine Sea a scant couple of hundred miles off the North New Guinea coast where his father would be mired in swamps or ascending into some mountainous rainforest.

During his research Bertie began a correspondence with an Englishman who had had a near-miss first contact with an unknown tribe in Northwest New Guinea. The prospect of stumbling across such a people in the fastness of the Fojas excited him. It is possible, he thought. Maybe in those deep ravines, or on the slopes of the knife-edge ridges, or perhaps on a plateau atop a sheer cliff. Who can say what's up there in that forest, hiding in those cloud banks? He thought to himself. Those people would live a stone-age existence, because iron would be unknown to them. What do they think I wonder, seeing a jet aircraft flying high above them, its white contrails lacing the sky? Can you imagine them!, he exclaimed to himself- looking up through the moss-clad canopy, seeing the spectacle of those contrails? Bertie was captivated now. His thoughts raced. That Englishman's near-miss two years ago prove they exist! And how would they react to him? Shunning contact? Or would they treat him as human prey? They may be nomadic, Bertie thought, shifting from one hunting ground to another. A small party, Bertie speculated, in this case he alone, stood a good chance of stumbling across something. For him, the prospect had set his imagination afire.

He studied the nature of game trails, as these scant traces would be the only tracks in an otherwise trackless wilderness. The navigational problem in those mountains was a formidable one, as there were no maps and no visible landmarks. He would navigate by compass and shooting azimuths for his course. Following the reciprocals of those azimuths was vital as he descended out of the mountains- otherwise he would become hopelessly lost.

On the verge of departure, Carolina had turned her back on him. And Claire had in effect done the same. He once told Claire that he missed the way she made him smile. Now, it looked as if she were lost to him forever. In any event, Claire had always maintained an inviolable sanctuary around herself, into which Bertie was prohibited entry. Whilst inside this fortress her silence became impenetrable. These twin losses, as Bertie regarded them, crushed his spirit. He was grimly determined to carry out his mission successfully, but now a seed of doubt was planted in his mind about his own chances: he now was plagued with the dangerous thought that he had no one to come back to. This was nonsense on the surface of it- he had a wonderful son to live for, with a grandchild on the way. But the nagging doubts he had learned to live with were somehow reinforced by his rejection by both women. The answer he devised was simply to immerse himself in the detailed planning of the trip, and to otherwise submerge all other emotion; and by a sheer force of will to give the appearance of a man too busy to care about anything else. And, in truth, the preparations were burden enough to occupy most of his waking time. And that is exactly what happened. Bertie became what he had been before he got to know Claire well: a brooding, silent, and seemingly indifferent man. But with one difference- he was consumed now by a single overarching objective. That was to find the crew of the Photo Queen.

With time, the immersion in the Expedition and his medical practice buoyed his spirits. He wrote Claire: "appetite and weight increasing, training momentum accelerating, on time and on target." The two of them met weekly to organize detailed planning in a stepwise fashion with a Checklist. Claire, with her usual relentless nagging, kept Bertie on track, and they briefed each other on each key step in the plan. And she kept him smiling with her mock insults, and at times Bertie even managed to bring out laughter in her with some mutual playful farce. And she plainly enjoyed making him laugh out loud at a string of mocking observations at his ineptness at organizing papers. Her periodic use of colloquialisms amazed him again and again: she was going to "scope" something out, or called him "chief",

He told her the use of these peculiar slang words was long out of fashion, and it was her seemingly unlimited fund of words or expressions that continually amazed him. Bertie had realized that in many ways they were well suited to each other, and it was this knowledge that actually caused him painful moments, because he cursed the fact that they were not together in a permanent sense; and he had a deep, wounding feeling of loss, of lost years, of memories lost, of their separation. The time they spent together was all too brief, and he missed her so much that at times her absence tore at his very fabric. He tried mightily to ward off that terrible feeling that they would never be true friends and lovers. He simply refused to accept it. But his refusal seemed to do nothing to change reality. When together organizing his papers, she avoided looking at him even when he spoke to her. There were stretches of time when she would remain utterly silent, a state that was by now habitual. The playfulness in her seemed to just vanish. Indeed, normal conversation was at a premium. And he could not fathom why.

Claire had changed so much in the past year it exasperated and saddened Bertie. And he knew that in large part it was because of the daily grind she was put through every day of the week. Three children, two jobs, cooking, cleaning- it must be exhausting he thought. Bertie wanted so much to help her, but had very few, if any, ways to do it. He maintained an informal work relationship with her, always thinking of ways he could ease her burdens at work. He felt he should do all he could to come to her aid. The truth was he spoiled her and enjoyed doing it.

Above all he longed for a chance to just talk things out with her. Not just to hash the whole thing over, but to ask her to turn back the clock as it were. Resume that comfortable feeling they had once had- even now there were times it surfaced- before love and all its vagaries and volatility got in the way. Not seemingly ever to have her alone for such a talk, he resorted to a letter pouring out his frustration. He knew it was probably useless, as she would ignore it. Worse than that, he regretted even sending it. And she may well be right in doing so, he thought finally. After all, given a little patience, he figured, things will just turn out ok.

And so, the erstwhile Hunter, Bertie, went on preparing for his walk in the sun. And as to any thoughts on his odds? Would the Hunter come home from the hills? He had banished them for now-time was indeed running out as another Thanksgiving ended.

Drifting

"Sometimes, well more than sometimes really, I find myself adrift, rudderless, at the whim of the currents, forced to allow these merciless currents to take me where they will. No longer sailing free with a brisk wind at my back, shipping green water over my bows, and with no stinging, exhilarating salt spray slapping my face and bringing me alive.

Waiting. Waiting for you to throw me a lifeline, then pulling me to you, holding me fast, never to let me drift way again. "Waiting for daybreak" as I once put it. But you make no move; you give me no hope of rescue. It is as if whatever you think of me is so harsh and pitiless that you disdain me. Once you said to me that I was crazy, and you meant it, and it wounded me.

I am far from unbalanced. Think of it in this way: everything I said to you, or did, or wrote for you- it was all done because of love. Perhaps then you would not judge me so harshly. I am not crazy. I am just an ordinary man, not unlike other men.

Except, I am a man who loved you."- extract from a letter from Bertie to Claire.

Charade

"They asked me how I knew
My true love was true.
I, of course, replied:
Something here inside cannot be denied.

They said "Someday you will find all who love are blind";
When your heart's on fire
You must realize, smoke gets in your eyes.

So, I laughed, I gaily laughed,
To think they could doubt my love.
Yet, today, my love has flown away;
I am without my love.

Now, laughing friends deride
Tears I cannot hide.
So, I smile and say:
When a lovely flame dies,
Smoke gets in your eyes."- From the song by Jerome Kern and Otto
Harbach.

"I want you to fool me. Trick me. Pretend. Pretend you really love me after all. Humor me. But do it in such a way that I will forget it's just a charade, if that is what it really is. You know how to do it. A little kindness here, a little warmth there. After all, I'm one of those suckers born every minute- an easy mark. Don't give me an even break. Just an old fool who doesn't know the difference. Look at it any way you want to, just make it convincing. It's the only chance I've got, you know. When I'm overseas I can tell myself, I've got to come back, because I'm coming back to you.

Maybe one day let me feel the touch of your hand. Maybe surprise me with a hug and a kiss right out of the blue. Call me endearing names again, just like you did last year. You remember those wonderful names, don't you? You know what to do. Or we will just sit there looking into each other's eyes without saying a word, just like we did on that day last year. Maybe then, at that moment, you will let your feelings for me escape from where you buried them inside you. Maybe this time you will open the door and let me in- you will let me see the light in your eyes, you will let me feel your warmth.

And this time, we will hold each other. This time it will not be a charade."- Letter from Bertie to Claire.

A Time To Mourn

Bertie had been preoccupied more and more with the upcoming Expedition. Each time he went through the checklist of preparation with Claire, he allowed his mind to ponder the odds. And he began to become obsessed with the numerous dangers that might befall him. It was unlike him to take counsel of his fears, when in similar circumstances in the past. He had simply immersed himself in plans and their execution, missions and objectives, and giving attention to detail, all in the effort to defeat the enemy. Now he must do the same. One evening after work in the office he confided in Claire.

I wonder, he told her, if I can do this again and come through. Whatever I may have done before, it was so long ago. You know, you wonder- maybe I lost my edge. Can I win through really, succeed in actually doing what I set out to do? How many times can you go to the well and get away with it? One misstep, a run of bad luck- that's all it takes, you know. Is my number up? That question keeps nagging me. But then I say to myself what did you tell your men when one of them might think his number was up? You told them most guys who think that way turn out ok. And what if your number is really up? So, what. You can't do anything about it. You have got to sweep your fears aside for a while, put your fears to bed, then go out and do the job you came here to do. Why, that's the essence of what we call courage.

Claire, I can tell you now, nothing is going to stop me; I can't be beaten! I'm going to do the job I have to do. Nobody thinks much of my chances. Well, I don't much care if this is the Last Hurrah. Any one of us, no, all of us, has only a finite time on this good earth, and sometimes you've got to make it count for something. Sometimes you've got to make a stand. Well I stand on this: I'm going to find those men and make certain they get back here, where they belong-home; no matter what happens to me later in those mountains. Claire, I've just got to ask you- do you believe in me? Not do you believe me, but do you believe IN me? She unhesitatingly answered: "Yes, I do." He began to sense almost right away that Feeling begin to wash over him. He quickly embraced her and, tenderly and slowly, kissed her on her cheek. It was an unthinking spontaneous act. He said nothing more, just pulled back and, his hands still clinging to her shoulders, looked into her eyes and smiled. Her reaction to all this was just to say to him: "Gosh, don't worry so much." It was typical of her- just to reduce a problem to its simplest solution; she was the master of the finality of brevity, cutting to the heart of a dilemma, in this case his dilemma, quickly.

Later, after she had gone, he sat in his chair, virtually immobile. He felt the Feeling envelop him completely. It was if he was safely surrounded by a protective cocoon. The Feeling stayed with him long after he returned home. Yes, he said to himself, I am going to do it.

But then the foray south into the mountains intruded- he would go there to follow his boyhood dream of being a true explorer, walking into the unknown. Why, there was even the possibility of discovering an unknown tribe there, one without any previous contact with the outside world. But no one, not him, not anyone, knew what might await him there.

Yes, it was there, he thought, where fate would truly become the hunter. And then would there come the time to mourn?

Heartlight

"Why would you take away one of the few things I have left? After I have given up. It doesn't make a whit of difference anymore, yet you deny it to me. A man has to have something, some cherished memories, otherwise you kill everything inside him. It is as if you set out to destroy my love for you that I have anchored inside of me. As if it were a great crime to love you. That is not you; you are not cruel, or don't mean to be. Out of sheer contrariness you called me deluded. Sleep deprivation affected you that day, you said. I do not buy that for a second. Thou dost protest too much. If you set out to destroy my feelings for you, you are doing a good job of it. But, no, that is not you. It's too artificial, it's unnatural. And you would never knowingly do that to me. Then what is it that makes you appear cold? You won't tell me the truth, but I know the answer anyway: you have been suppressing your own emotions. And, of course you must stick to your decision, and not encourage me. But you need not worry any longer- I have already called it quits.

You loved me that day, in those moments, and now you persist in this scorched earth policy because you dare not let your feelings for me escape again, nor can you allow me any hope. I have seen and felt your true warmth and tenderness. You once told me "thank you for thinking of me". That came from your heart. All those endearing things you gave me that brought on the Feeling in me, they were all born in your heart. And when you turn on your heart-light for me- you bring a smile to my face and an utter peace to my soul. If this is all I will have left, then it will be enough.

When I am gone away, Claire, keep your heart-light shining for me always. We will now forever be apart, but it will matter not how far away from you I am, nor how long ago my memories of you are. I will turn and look back, and I will see and feel your heart-light: burning bright."- extract from a letter by Bertie to Claire.

It was written after a contentious time spent together after work one evening. Claire had just denied that the two of them had any feelings for each other. She had walked out on him during one of his feeble attempts to talk things out with her. Bertie had failed once again to overcome his shyness and organize his thoughts, and Claire had angrily departed.

Why?

"The woods are lovely, dark and deep.
But I have promises to keep,
And miles to go before I sleep,
And miles to go before I sleep". - Robert Frost.

"Someone might ask, why? Why are you going to go? Why take the risk?
And I give this answer, about the men who were lost:

"He stands in the unbroken line of patriots who have
Dared to die that freedom might live, and grow, and
Increase its blessings. Freedom lives, and through it he lives-
In a way that humbles the undertakings of most men". - Harry S.
Truman.

I know more than anyone what I am walking into.
Why do we do any of the things that life calls on us to do?

I've got to try.
I've just got to try."- extract from Bertie's diary, sent to both Carolina
and Claire.

Tink

He said goodbye to her for the last time just before leaving for the Academy. Like all living things she had been overtaken by the years and was in the final stage of her long life. Tinkerbell, as she had been named by him 17 years before, was just a Mutt- sleek and fast and absolutely loyal to him. She died in the fall of his First-Class year; he away at the School, as the Academy was euphemistically called by its young inmates. He grieved for her silently.

Bertie's Grandfather made a coffin for the dog and his Father picked out a quiet spot on the edge of some woods bordering the backyard. The chiseled piece of stone marking the grave gave the dog's name and dates.

Bertie had last visited the place nine years earlier. Now, on the brink of his departure for New Guinea, he went again. He stood there, hands in pockets, reading the simple inscription in the stone. He recalled with great fondness their almost daily forays into the forests- he, merely a boy of eleven years and she perhaps in her prime at eight years of age.

"Exploring!" he would emphatically declare to his Mother, when asked where they were off to. And then the two companions would quickly and happily disappear into and beyond the tree line, and not return for hours. During this period of time they wandered for several miles usually on a constant bearing, and returning on a reciprocal heading, even though Bertie had no idea of the meaning of these terms. Even at this early age he seemed to have instinctively grasped the need for going forward on a uniform course and coming back in the same path. Even when deviating from the main heading to check into some interesting terrain feature that caught his eye, he always returned to his base course. Purposefully the boy carefully memorized the game trails; crossed a wide stream he promptly christened "Tinkerbell Creek" and catalogued all the likely hiding spots where they could conceal themselves quietly should anyone else come across their path, and they sometimes used these hideouts-lying motionless together as someone passed down their trail. The dog somehow knew barking was forbidden and remained by Bertie's side, absolutely still and silent. The boy constantly kept an eye on his dog, who, being a natural hunting dog, would "point" as these dogs do by instinct when spotting a deer or other creature of the forest. She would also point if humans were near, long before Bertie could spot them. Even with deer if the boy commanded her to lie motionless, she would obey him.

He stood by the old grave for perhaps thirty minutes silently, just remembering all their youthful adventures together. Then he said, to himself and to his dog aloud: "Well, I'm off exploring again, Tink, next week. I know you can't go this time, and I wish to God you could be with me again. This time maybe I can name a river for you." He hesitated just a few seconds, and said "Goodbye, Tink." He turned and strode quickly away.

He was surprised to discover the tears welling up in his eyes.

Alone?

"It is a far, far better thing I do than I have ever done.
It is a far, far better rest I go to than I have ever known". - From A
Tale of Two Cities by Charles Dickens.

"Just recently, four months before my projected departure for New
Guinea, Carolina said not to expect her to say goodbye, just get in
the taxi and go. I imagined it to be a turning of her back on me
when I left.

This threat, and Claire's seeming coldness toward me at times,
began to convince me that what I feared most was underway:
emotional isolation. Being over sensitive and melodramatic, I think
this way sometimes- and I begin to adopt the persona of Dicken's
character D'Evremonde as he mounts the scaffold of the Guillotine.
Then I become downhearted in the worst way. And as often as not,
I make a big deal out of nothing, or the two of them will take notice
and act in some way to alleviate my fears.

In Claire's case, all personal traces of our relationship had been
removed by her. All that remained was a formal and sterile and

cold relationship. I cannot fault her nor blame her in any way, but I did not understand, I did not understand why, anymore. She had become a completely different person with me than she was just one year ago; it was like night and day, a stark contrast. As a rule, she neither spoke to me nor looked at me when we were together. She would do her job in the usual thorough fashion, then depart as quickly as possible. There must be a compelling reason for all this, but I cannot fathom it, only speculate. It must be one of two things. I say to myself 'She must not care for me very much; she must dislike me very much. Let's be honest, I must be honest with myself: she does not care at all about me; it matters not to her what happens to me.' Or she still cares a great deal for me, still has feelings for me, and won't let them show. Indeed, that is why she has resorted to such extreme behavior towards me. But it really makes no difference at all, the end result is the same- she, too, will have turned her back on me. Yet we become closer again, comfortable with each other again, just as it was, just a few days later. Maybe it is because I don't press her any more, and she responds by being more natural with me- the personal touch she had with me is still missing, though. And only when the time comes will it be known how both of them really see me off. I know only that I would be devastated if I could not say my farewells to them both, separately and in private. Yet the last thing I want to do is give them any cause for worry.

And Carolina is entirely correct about one thing: I am temporarily giving up my primary responsibility, my responsibility to her. But an old duty calls me now. I had in effect given my word to my grandfather to try to find Uncle Jim. Now, at long last, I must keep my word. Words are what men live by, and I must try. I have got to give it my best, regardless of the risks. And I have tried to have she and I fall in love with each other again, without much success. She did tell me she loved me again, after so many years. Maybe that is a start.

My love for both women is not diminished. I have accepted things as they are in regard to Claire. I have accepted that it is too late for us. I have renewed my bond to Carolina. Yet both relationships seem at times to lie in tatters. I can only chalk that up to the shifting moods of women, and their, at times, capricious behavior. As for myself, the feelings of love, once embedded in me, can never be thrown out- those feelings stay with me, and I am now sure those feelings stay with both Carolina and Claire. The two of them are very much alike, and neither would admit that it is true they still have deep feelings toward me. But they both love me, of that I am certain. Not that they won't turn up the heat and really press me when D-Day gets close- then I can expect them to really let me have it, with both barrels.

So, what if I get the feeling sometimes, when I depart, I will be truly and completely alone. No one will wish me farewell, no goodbyes, no embraces: isolation. And nothing much to come back to. An unhealthy attitude, and an ignorant one as well. And it is groundless to boot. These good women will never isolate me. I've told Carolina and Tracy, my Nurse for thirty years, and I will repeat it for Claire: this is just another "walk in the sun"; I've taken plenty of those walks and I've always come back. Don't sweat it, girls. They all seemed to gang up on me at the same time. Tracy was fighting back tears, telling me I had no business doing this at my age. Claire simply and abruptly said demandingly, "You are not going, you know that. You won't make it"- too used to the easy life, she threw in for good measure. Carolina, just as Claire, slammed me with "You are not coming back, you know." My mother in law, Mami, said I am too used to my comforts. The point is, these women sometimes speak up in odd ways when they worry a great deal about me, when they see great danger to me. They are trying to stop me, and to tell me in their own way that they love me. And they all have touched me deeply. I was almost shocked at the depth of their feelings. And I must say it warms my heart; at the same time, I know I must find a way to ease their fears.

Tracy is another case in point. Being together so many years in the office, that at one point she said it was like having two husbands.

We have had the same contentious then friendly relations that make up a marriage. Come to think of it, Carolina and then Claire have both taken me on that same roller coaster ride. Very recently, Tracy and I have become accepting and quite comfortable with each other. There are no more emotionally wrenching disagreements. We have grown closer together than ever before. Before leaving for Florida for a few months, she surprised me with a very tight embrace and then a desperate kiss.

Despite all the bad feelings I have had from time to time, hatched in moments of despair, somehow, I know that they do love me, that they worry about me, that they fear I may not survive. And I will always think of them as warm-hearted, wonderful women who gave me the happiest days of my life. Alone? No. They will never allow me to go away feeling that I am alone. At the close of each day that remains to me when I am over there, when the quick tropical darkness envelops my camp, I will see their faces. And I will hear their voices.

And I will smile."- extract from Bertie's diary.

What Price, Glory?

"Some men see things as they are and ask 'Why?'.
I dream dreams that never were, and ask 'Why
not'. - George Bernard Shaw.

T.E. Lawrence had written in Seven Pillars of Wisdom that it was
the dreamers by day who were the dangerous dreamers. And Bertie
was one of them. He chased rainbows and tilted at windmills his
entire life. He found joy and pride in an endless supply of radical
schemes and revolutionary dreams that periodically emerged from
his infinite imagination. His keen intellect forged these flights of
fancy into concrete plans of action, most of which fizzled out, as
often as not because he lost interest in them. One of his professors at
the Academy told him he was "brilliant but jaded". The price of his
latest dream lay in the wreckage of his marriage, the helpless worry
inflicted upon his son, and the by now firm conviction of Claire that
he could be written off as crazy. Crazy, to him, meant he was less
than a man and that opinion had been like a knife thrust into his
vitals, causing him unrelenting anguish. The view of him as insane

was shared by his wife, who had also questioned his manhood on more than one occasion.

There was in him a yearning for some new adventurous exploit. And New Guinea filled the bill. The explosive mixture of a true catechism of idealism and a thinly concealed quest for glory, carried with it a terrible price. In the end, he now realized, it could very well cost him his life. His youth now gone, he had lost more than just a step. Although this gave him pause, it would not deter him. He only lamented the emerging probability that there would be no farewells, no chance to finally give voice to any regrets, and to at last declare in full measure his genuine love to both women. Bertie's boundless capacity to shower them with affection might very well be denied.

The Expedition was justifiably viewed as foolhardy by everyone, and, with six weeks to go, Bertie now agreed with them. With a fanatical zeal he threw himself into strict attention to detail, just as he had done during the war. With the odds nearly hopeless, he began to devise ways to cut them down. Publicly he engaged in, or put up with, stock jokes about head-hunters, crocodiles, and snakes. Privately, he knew the places he was going to were far more dangerous than anyone realized. He set about devising contingency plans with sub-plans within them, striving mightily to foresee problems and threats he might run into, and improvising ways to adapt to them and overcome them. Yet he also knew just plain luck would play a significant role in his survival or demise. His grinding study of the true nature of New Guinea revealed to him a grim panoply of mortal dangers. He would attempt to obtain a hunting license in order to be able to carry a rifle- a sure sign of the peril now facing him. And above all he studied the terrain and the job he was going to do, pouring over aerial photos, maps and the social structure and spiritual beliefs of the Tribes. In all the welter of tasks he kept his attention fixed on the objective: find Photo Queen and its crew.

In spite of her opinion of his scheme, Claire helped him in her practical way, to keep him on course, and even at key points to boost his morale. One Sunday, while he sat working in his office, he sent her a progress report on his "chores" as she called them. She replied by sending him "Good Boy". He laughed aloud at that, and for days he was still smiling whenever he thought of her message. She had said this to him often in the past, but she hadn't uttered the phrase in months. It was one of those personal things between them that had vanished.

There is a parable that intruded itself into Bertie's thoughts on another of those lonely evenings on his veranda. A Roman Centurion was being showered with accolades from the adoring citizens of Rome on his return from some new conquest in far off Africa. Much to his surprise, the Oracle of Rome suddenly appeared in his chariot beside him. The Oracle leaned over and whispered in his ear:

"Remember Centurion, all Glory is fleeting"

We Shall Not Pass
This Way Again

".... And let no chance be lost
To kindness show at any cost.
I shall not pass this way again.
Then let me now relieve some pain,
Remove some barrier from the road,
Or lighten someone's heavy load....

For those who bear their burdens all alone,
A larger kindness gives to me,
A deeper love....

Then one day
May someone say
Would she could pass this way again."-adapted from" I Shall Not
Pass This Way Again" by Eva Rose York.

Bertie's wife was right on the edge of desperation. Carolina threatened divorce, told him he wasn't coming back- he was going to die there she told him. Two days later, with 61 days left until he departed for the Southwest Pacific, she said the stress was getting to him. Carolina went so far as to ask Claire to intervene by asking Bertie personally to stay. But Claire declined, saying he was too determined to go. What Carolina could not know was Bertie had once told Claire "If you asked me to stay, I would not know what to do". Carolina really loves me, he thought, putting on the full court press now to stop me. Or is it the scandal she fears and the terribly difficult days that would ensue should I disappear? Maybe all of these. Of this he was certain: as the days dwindled, he would be, no they both would be, squeezed through an emotional wringer. In the end, they would both feel as if they had been abandoned. Then the bond of real love that held them together would be shattered. Drifting apart, Carolina angry, Bertie drowning in sorrow, the capricious currents of fate would draw them further from each other.

Bertie's optimistic feeling that the women in his life would never let him leave emotionally isolated now began to crumble under a plethora of doubt. Claire persisted in her refusal to allow any closeness between them to evolve. She relentlessly forbade any personal ties to penetrate the fortress of silence she had erected around herself and her children. She had even ceased apprising him of the young Max progress in milestones. And she had found real or imagined faults in him that provided justification for her keeping him at arm's length- indeed it made her artificial task of isolating herself from him far easier. What Bertie feared most was happening: Claire had now converted her conscious effort to deny him anything that could be construed as closeness into an almost habitual liturgy of silence and distance. For him, at times, it had driven him to fitfully lose his faith in her essential goodness, only to briefly regain it by some outpouring of her old, natural self toward him- these moments or, rarely, evenings, of camaraderie he had come to think of as her rescue of him from the depths of despair into which he had descended. It was a roller coaster ride with which he was all too familiar. But the reprieves she gave him became fewer and less clear-cut. And then he would be plunged once again into an almost atheistic doubt, with bitterness surfacing its ugly head once more. Then seeing her again only rekindled the flames of his affection- it was Just One Look all over again. Thus, he waited in vain for her to reverse course.

He finally resolved to appeal to her to once again open her heart to him. To give them both some measure of tenderness. Without this, he feared only a haunting regret would remain. He said to her he could not shake the feeling that "time is running out on us. And when it does it may be too late for anything." Claire seemed momentarily stunned by what he had vouchsafed to her. She almost immediately knew what he meant- that it was more than just possible he might not return from New Guinea.

Two weeks later, it was Bertie who reversed course. He had been brooding. For a day or two he dwelled on what he now believed was his probable death. His recent discoveries changed everything: the violent, boiling cauldron that would confront him in the Gorges of the MAMBERAMO River; at long last pinpointing the location of the strange village of the AER MATI people and the bizarre appearance of it, with its abandoned airstrip and its remoteness from any other village. The bursts of irrational violence- murders, sorcery, the burning alive of suspected witches; a marginal note from a map he had obtained, declaring the Natives at his starting point to ascend the MAMBERAMO River to be "cannibalistic"; the stark, wild and rugged appearance of the mist-choked FOJA Mountains. He resolved to tell Claire to let the whole thing go, no more reminders about things to do to get ready, to forget it. It's better that way, he told himself- he didn't want her to have anything to do with the Expedition. And that was that. No more discussion, no more jokes, no more mention of it. Just get ready then go. He decided it was altogether better to be "here today and gone tomorrow, not a trace left behind" after all. And that meant no Goodbyes, no moments laden with emotion. That way no one would feel responsible if "stuff happened".

So, ironically, Bertie was now trying to isolate himself, to put up a wall between everyone and himself. It would be easier for them all if they we're to just continue to see him as a lunatic. Throwing himself into a frenzy of preparation, adopting a hitherto uncharacteristic cold-blooded persona, could only serve to confirm that view of him. At the close of day, Bertie sat on the veranda reading from his old reconstructed journal. In the entry for April 1963 he had written: "Grandpa and me reading "one of our favorite poems", as he put it." On the journal page was a poem by Edmund Vance Cooke. Its title was "How Did You Die?" Bertie silently read the last verse

"…. It isn't the fact that you're licked that counts'
Its how did you fight —and why?..
And though you be done to death, what then?
If you battled the best you could,
If you played your part in the world of men,
Why, the Critic will call it good.
Death comes with a crawl, or comes with a pounce,
And whether he's slow or spry,
It isn't the fact that you're dead that counts,
But only how did you die."

Bertie looked up and exhaled slowly, then aloud he said:
"If you played your part in the world of men……."
"How did you fight; how did you die…….and Why?"

Portrait

As was his habit each Sunday, Bertie was in his office going through a thick folder of lab results, consult letters, patient problems, and phone call requests. An hour into his ritual he turned a page over and in doing so suddenly realized the next item was a photo paper turned upside down. He turned it over and looked at it with a blank stare, trying to comprehend what he was seeing. Why, it's a photograph, he thought. Of what? Then, in an instant, he went from confused to stunned. It was a 5x7 photograph of Claire, professionally done. A portrait, really, he thought, a portrait of a lady, and a woman, all rolled into one. And it is perfect, he marveled to himself. She was smiling and those bright green eyes seemed to be looking right at him. The blonde hair was styled exactly the way he preferred it to be. Her face revealed anticipation and a little apprehension, he thought; it showed a worry that perhaps the picture was not good enough, that he would not like it, that he would be disappointed. She need not to have been worried, he said to himself. It was the eyes that mesmerized him, those eyes in which he had once told her he had become lost. But it just didn't figure, somehow. Why, she had always insisted he would not receive it until he returned from New Guinea.

He stopped wondering immediately. He tried and failed to continue his work. It was futile- that almost Indefinable Feeling began to overcome him. He was impelled to move to a side chair and remained there, letting the sensation of that Feeling wash over him. As if he were enveloped in an invisible, impenetrable canopy, the chaotic cacophony of the world outside suddenly rendered mute. The peace and tranquility inside his canopy was at the same time of an intensity that deepened by the minute and endured. He did not know how long he remained there, looking at the photograph and believing all was right with the world.

The Feeling would not ebb out of him until sleep finally erased it late that evening. Two days later he went to her home to help young Charlie with his homework. When they were done, and the children were out of the kitchen, Bertie stood next to Claire. He said only one thing- "I don't have the words; I just don't have the words." Then he kissed her on her cheek and let his lips linger there for a time before she pulled away from him. He told her about the Feeling being restored to him, eliciting a kind of sigh from her, the meaning of which he could not decipher. In a soft voice he said to her "It was the first time I have had it since you sent me that first Nighty-night." At that, she emitted that mysterious sigh again, and gently hurried him to the door, perhaps sensing what this might be leading to. He protested briefly about her pushing him away, but she overrode him with a rejoinder- "I must get the kids to their activities", and that mollified him.

The last Sunday he would have before he departed to cross the Pacific, he was back in his office once again. He retrieved the now framed photograph from his desk drawer, unwrapped it, and placed it on the desk to his left. Then he commenced his usual Sunday work. He would pause only briefly over the next two hours to glance at the photo, but when he finally put away the last patient chart, he leaned a little forward and allowed his gaze to come to rest upon her visage. After just a few minutes the Feeling began again, this time with far less intensity. He sat stock still for several minutes, then, reluctantly, he carefully wrapped up his prize and returned it to its place in the desk drawer- he had a House Call to make. He had resolved never to allow anyone to see it- it would remain a private matter between Claire and himself. A few days later he showed her the ways in which he preserved the photo and told her of his determination to jealously guard the privacy of it. Claire grinned and emitted a soft string of quiet laughter, looking at Bertie all the while, the grin transformed now into a continuous smile, the smile persisting after the mirthful, soft laughter had ceased. She placed her hands on the desk, one on top of the other, then gently lowered her face on them, and looked up at him, smiling. And so, for a moment she just gazed at him with that smile. She was amused by the seriousness in his expression, and yet she also found his pride of purpose to be charming and even reassuring. He simply marveled at her attentiveness towards him- she had seldom ever before fixed her attention upon him, much less smiled at him for so long a time. He could not have been more pleased, and it showed. He smiled at her, too, in that brief moment. Although Bertie would never fully accept that he was fated to never consummate his desire to marry Claire, he steadfastly maintained his love for his wife, though she made this difficult to do much of the time. Her desire for a separation or divorce was periodically voiced, then dropped. At these intervals he would take the weight of guilt upon himself and issue a mea culpa. That he was capable of loving two women at the same time, never struck him as a contradiction. Moreover, with Claire now apparently firm in her conviction not to allow him to draw too close to her, he dispensed with much of his open expression of his affection for her. But Bertie was incapable of suppressing his feelings entirely. Indeed, he had been guided by his heart far more often than not his entire life. Even during the War, when he transformed himself into a relatively coldly calculating leader, in decisive moments he was often swept up in an emotional firestorm of naked fury, inspiring and driving his men to carry the day.

Bertie had, by this time, reached a point of frustration. His desire to be physically close to Claire, though the nearness of her gave him a measure of happiness, cut two ways, and was always too short a time, inevitably casting him into sadness when she left him. And even during those times, he was denied what he felt was missing- open verbal and physical demonstration of his love for her and she for him. He was forced to stand or sit by her and just take it. There were moments when he felt he just couldn't take it any longer- he wanted so badly to put his arms around her, to feel her pressing up against him, to tell her how deeply his love for her resided in him. When these moments became unbearable, he had sometimes just left abruptly, tossing off a "See you around", and not looking back. More often, he would just swallow the disappointment whole and bid her a friendly adieu, pausing only to kiss the kid's goodbye. And he buried these disappointments inside, not divulging them openly to her. He now sensed it would make no difference. He would often fall back on an all too easy way of avoiding further thinking about it, saying to himself "That's just the way it is". Yet Claire, he knew, could read the dejection in his face and eyes, and would in turn briefly look at him with a look of alarm and worry for him- she instinctively wanted to help him, but would not allow herself to say or do anything to lift the burden from him, and she would painfully look away, hurt written on her face, hurt because she felt she could not permit herself to ease that burden. She would many times studiously avoid looking at him out of fear that she might give in to her own desires, so intent was she to stick to her decision to stay the course of her marriage. Yet there were unguarded moments when she wavered, and gave in. After they had spent a rare day together, about to say goodbye again, she came to him and they warmly embraced, their bodies firmly pressing against each other, if even for a brief moment. Her action surprised Bertie; as they parted, he stood frozen in amazement. But when she and Bertie were not together, which was most of the time, she seldom thought of him, so beset was she by the demands of her life. Eventually she was able, by the way of habit, to dismiss him from her thoughts completely. She no longer messaged him to ask how he was doing, nor did she ever again complain to him that she hadn't heard from him. Her emails to him had long before ceased entirely. His emails to her went unanswered, and so he stopped sending them. Her silence was probably the most distressful thing to him for a while, and then it became the most hurtful. It caused in him some of the worst downhearted episodes he had ever experienced. Yet he retained a small gleam of hope she might someday change her mind. That minuscule flame of hope was all he had left to stave off an utter emptiness within him. For once a man is shorn of hope, the feelings that have dwelled within him for so long are destroyed, and nothing remains but his memories. If these are taken from him, then an emptiness of spirit fills the vacuum and despair will overcome him.

But now, Bertie was all too aware that the clock was ticking off the hours, maybe his last hours, and so too by now was Claire. She visibly lightened up on him, not quite flinging open the door she had shut on him more than a year before, but the door was cracked open now. He sensed from her behavior that now she would listen to him, not walk away if he wanted to open up and tell her how he felt.

On the way home he wondered yet again about the timing of her gift. He quite suddenly thought of her reason for the abrupt reversal in giving it to him now:

Claire now truly believed he might not ever return from New Guinea. She had even assented to giving him time alone with her the following week. As Bertie turned in that night, the clock moved past midnight. There were now only seven days left.

Wistfully Yours

"The night has a thousand eyes,
The day but one;
Yet the light of the bright world dies
With the dying sun.

The mind has a thousand eyes,
And the heart but one;
Yet the light of a whole life dies
When love is done"- Francis Bourdillon.

Reflections on Daydreams.

The eyes see forever, lost in thought, wistful, with lids somewhat heavy, eyes deep dreamy pools of blue or green. Yet the eyes see nothing, and the mind sees from here to eternity. Almost as if in mourning or drowning in grief or stricken by longing or brimming with desire or stunned by regret. They dream dreams of what might have been, and then softly and silently shed their tears of loss, weeping alone.

The eyes mourn for what they have lost; they grieve for that which will never be. Longing will be denied, desire will be unfulfilled, love will be unrequited, regrets will embitter. And the eyes will pleadingly ask why must this be so, but their pleas will be in vain, and they will forever be unanswered.

Awakening from their reverie, the eyes now have only a small measure of sparkle left. Although the lids open wide, there is in those pools now only a desperate sorrow. In time, perhaps a hard edge will form around the eyes, to shield them from future hurt. But it is too late. The pain will never leave them- it is a pain of loss and a wound that will never heal because of that which will never be:

You and I together. You and I.
Once, the nearness of you made my eyes gleam.
Once, you made me smile.

*   *   *

Memories.

He was just looking at her. Only have eyes for you. She was standing on the other side of the open partition window, shuffling some papers. Then as she glanced upward, their eyes met. Once again, they now just stood looking at each other. Her eyes searched his, and she quickly realized his eyes were beseeching her, pleading with her. There was no intensity in her visage this time. Instead, suddenly her eyes softened, became gentle, then seemed to fill with a longing to help him, to come to him, to love him. But with an almost painful regret she looked down as if the regret were a weight pressing her head downward. She stood nervously and aimlessly fiddling with some objects, feigning busyness, in order to keep her eyes downcast- thus she did not have to look at him again. It was as if she was struggling to bottle up her feelings, her natural urge to come to his aid. As in January, neither had said a word. They had divined each other's thoughts simply by looking into each other's eyes.

Later, when he remembered this bitter-sweet moment, he would remember the gentleness of her soft green eyes, and their wistful sadness over that which would never be. In her heart, she wanted to love him, yet she felt she could not allow herself to do so. She could not allow the feelings she still harbored for him, somewhere inside her, to show. And he began to recall those precious memories of her when they had been together at any time or other.

He would remember watching her daydream one evening in late autumn, the baby cradled in her arms. Her vacuous, slightly hooded, verdant eyes seemed to see far away, wistfully dreaming, perhaps of what might have been. He remembered he had never seen her more beautiful than she was in those quiet moments.

He would remember how she visibly brightened when he came through the door. And she would smile for him, her eyes sparkling like green diamonds.

How, from the start, her bright green eyes captured him at any time they were close to each other, mesmerizing him to such an extent that he would later tell her he was lost in her eyes; lost to such a degree that any goings on around them just faded from his consciousness.

When she would rest her hand on his knee or shoulder and point out how the baby had discovered something new.

The utter peace that came over him, unlike anything in his lifetime, when she sent him that first "Nighty-night".

She, saying to him, when his Sister died, "I am thinking of you".

And he, saying to her in return, "Our God must be a good God, because He has put you on this Earth".

On his return from the funeral, her inscription in the children's welcome back notes: Love, Claire.

Simply talking with her on the telephone that December day in New York and taking delight in her admission she never wanted him to hang up.

Her mocking insults and endearing names she gave him, and then her bursts of happy laughter.

How, each time she drove off she would sound the horn, smile, and wave. And how he said to her the words of a song: "Every time we say goodbye, I die a little".

He would remember the intensity in her eyes that fateful, cold day in January.

And more than all of these, he would remember her promise to keep him in her heart always.

These cherished memories were destined to be all he had left, when time finally ran out, and he had gone away.

It is said there is a time to every purpose under heaven. For Claire and Bertie that time would never come. For Carolina and Bertie, that time would end.

Last Dance

"She hardly ever thought of him. He had worn a place for himself in some corner of her heart, as a seashell, always boring against a rock, might do. The making of the place had been her pain. But now the shell was safely in the rock. It ground no longer."- T.H. White, "The Once and Future King".

"Remember, I have always kept you
In my heart, and I have always
Prayed you would find. a little corner
Of your heart for me"- from the poem "Someday", the first ever written by Bertie for Claire.

"Save the last dance for me". These were the last words ever spoken by Bertie to Claire, and he said them with a smile. As the smile began to disintegrate, and pain began to fill his eyes, he turned and walked away. He had used this phrase several times when parting from her, and she had always smiled and laughed gaily at hearing them. On this occasion she did not smile. But, somewhere inside her, she knew he spoke this time out of sheer bravado, and that he was using the turn of phrase to conceal the heartbreak overcoming him: she had caught a glimpse of his pain. Knowing this, she herself felt emotion welling up in her, and found herself incapable of giving any more comfort to him than she already had. Having embraced each other one final time that moment of togetherness might be all they would ever have of each other. And Claire had promised Bertie once again to keep him in her heart always.

And so, Bertie faded out of her life, and she would once again be consumed by the relentless demands placed upon her. She buried him once again deep within. She would briefly resurrect him one Sunday in church, praying for his safe return. Yet the exigencies that she faced day after day demanded that her memories of him must be put on a shelf, and there, like the gifted poems and stories he wrote for her, gather the dust of neglect.

*   *   *

He had driven to her home to complete one last administrative detail. He was due to depart for New Guinea two days hence. The day before, Bertie had told her, that of all people she deserved to know the truth about New Guinea. Unlike other occasions when he spoke to her and she avoided eye contact, this time he had her full attention. He told her the truth, disclosing to her that there were three places there in which his fate would be decided by the flip of a coin, fifty-fifty odds of him getting through.

She was stunned by this, and it showed. During their work this new day he quite suddenly asked, "Claire, will you remember me?"

Claire mocked him at this seemingly foolish question, yet she was taken aback by the finality of it. She cocked her head to one side and leaned in toward him inquiringly to get a better look at him, in that way of hers when she was puzzled by him.

Then Bertie, in a poignant way, said to her: "If you do, if you think of me now and then, remember me for only one thing".

"What is that?", she asked.

He replied, "Remember me as the man who loved you".

Claire nodded twice, so affected by what he said that she could not speak.

When they were finished, they just sat at the table next to each other and he said, "You know something Claire, I'm going to win those three coin flips I told you about, and do you know why?"

When she answered No, he simply said "Unlucky in love, lucky in war".

She looked at him knowingly, then Bettie went on: "It's still the same old story, Claire, the fight for love and glory, a case of do or die" quoting from the lyrics of an old song. Then he told her, as if it were a prophecy, "When you've lost at love, the only thing left is Glory."

Claire's face registered alarm at this, and looked at him in a tender, silent plea to not let it be so. She had, some months before, decided to continue with the life she knew, with her children and husband, rather than coming together with Bertie. And Bertie had long since known this, and it tore at his heart and soul- he lived with the pain, but his longing for her never ceased. And she knew this.

And then it was time. Bertie stood up, saying "Well, I've got to shove off". Claire walked him to the door.

They paused at the door and looked at each other. Claire quickly closed the distance and put her arms around him, and they held each other. She held him close, and he buried his face in her neck. She said to him "Be safe. Come back to us. You better come back". Now, at a loss for words, he just said "Honey", and kissed her neck, evoking from her a half laugh, half sigh. Pulling away he kissed her again on her proffered cheek.

Once outside, he turned to her, put his arms around her and held her for just a moment. He whispered that he was going to miss her terribly. He kissed her yet again. Still in each other's arms he told her he loved her, and that he would always love her. She managed to tell him "Be good. Be safe". He pulled himself away from her, his hands still resting gently on her shoulders. She looked at him with those wide-open eyes, gazing straight into his, yet remained silent. But he once again saw the warmth and tenderness in her eyes. He had an overpowering urge to keep touching her, to hold on to her, as if he could not bear to walk away from her. He put his hand on her waist and squeezed her gently, smiling mischievously, and told her playfully "you're a lot of woman, Claire, and that's just the way I like it". She laughingly replied, smiling, "Oh, get out of here". Bertie stood silently with her for a few seconds, his hands still on her shoulders. Then he said to her in an even voice "I'm proud to have known you, Claire. And I'm proud to have loved you." He paused only briefly, then he told her "I will never forget. I'll never forget the way you made me smile.", and his voice began to break. Bertie turned as if to walk away, but he stopped himself and paused. Then, forcing a tortured smile, he said to her:

"Claire, save the last dance for me". Claire emitted a little cry at these words. Bertie did not see her fighting back the tears. He had turned away from her.

And then he was gone.

In Her Heart

"Somewhere in time,
One sunny morn,
We will awaken to find each other again.
Somewhere it will not be too late for us......

Where or when we cannot know,
Nor how we will find each other.
But it matters not,
For somewhere I will know your love,
And you, mine.

Somewhere in time." - From the poem of the same title, the last one ever written by Bertie for Claire.

The search for Photo Queen and its crew was at an end. Bertie broke Camp near the village of Kwerba as Morning Nautical Twilight came to its end and the sun peeked over the Northeastern horizon, bringing with it the sure promise of another hot day. As he packed away his gear, Bertie was silent, buried in his thoughts of what he had done so far, and thoughts of home- to him home was still an illusory place; his journey not yet finished. His now almost wistful thoughts turned to an inevitable vision. It was a vision of Claire. The ache he felt to hold her remained ever strong in him, even as he readied himself to journey even further from her.

He now thought more and more of what she had done for him. That Gift she gave, an indefinable feeling, had been restored to him. It was sublime, really. A stillness: no movement or noise penetrated the canopy of calm over him. A certain contentment: an armor protecting him from rage or rancor, from undue worry, from anything that thrust strife into his life.

In HEARTS AT PEACE he had said it set him sailing on a Sea of Feelings. If only he could somehow set, her a voyage on that same sea: give to her that Feeling. But that hope had proved elusive. Not that it was so important any longer. The cross of loneliness that he imagined he would bear alone had been lifted from his shoulders. His harsh judgments of her now were proved to have been fleeting. Before he left, she had come back to him, after all. She restored his smile, his laughter, his very well-being. She had done all these things- but still declined to return his love. And now, here in this wilderness into which he had exiled himself, his supposed unrequited love had not been rejected by her at all. With a sure sense of what she could give him, and what he would need to carry on, she gave him an eternal peace.

The seemingly futile hope of somewhere meeting again, somewhere where it would be not too late for them, was no longer just a dream. For that last gift she had given him had bound them together. Yes, of course, he realized now, it had joined them forever.

Bertie would now climb up into the forbidding Foja Mountains. He had long ago sensed what might await him there. His first and foremost duty was to get the search data for Photo Queen back to the States, along with his film and diary to date. He entrusted all of this to his Guide, Mac, to ship back to the States to Paul, his partner in the research to find Photo Queen. So here his Guide left him to journey down the Mamberamo River to the airhead at Kasonaweja. Bertie gave him one last request- to deliver a message via telegram to Claire. He pulled out a pen and a tore a blank page from his diary, wrote something down quickly and handed it to Mac. "It is important to me that you send this by Cable, Mac. Ask for confirmation." Mac nodded as Bertie handed him the folded paper. "Read it and tell me if you understand it". Mac answered yes and pledged to get everything through.

It said simply:
Somewhere in Time.

Bertie then shouldered his pack, saluted Mac, turned quickly, and, motioning to two Natives who would accompany him from Kwerba Village to the edge of their hunting grounds, disappeared into the jungle. Once just outside these hunting grounds the two Natives would turn back, and Bertie would ascend into the Mountains. He would be alone.

As he walked deeper into the jungle, bound for the high mist of the FOJA Mountains, he recalled her final boon that forged a bond between them which could never be sundered:

I am in her heart, he told himself- She put me there. That was the moment the Feeling was restored. She had helped to ease his pain, pain brought on by the thought of them never being together, of it being too late for them. He asked her to put him in her heart and to keep him there always, no matter what happened. She said "Yes, I will".

He had put her in his heart long ago, and he told her it was so. Perhaps that was it, he told himself. Yes, that was it. Both of them now safely sheltered, and in some way they would now always be together.

He came to the top of a rolling hill into a clearing. There, in the distance, patches of verdant green rainforest were shrouded in a white, almost diaphanous cloak- the unexplored and mostly unknown Fojas, seemed to rear up right in front of him- a massive green and white edifice. The green mass of rain forest stretched endlessly all the way to the far horizon, pure white billowing clouds cloaked the peaks, their streamers spilling across and down the ridges, ridges that marched in a procession as far as the eye could see. Either his Destiny or his Fate waited there, he thought. But now, staring vacantly at the white shroud in the distance, he saw the truth clearly.

Yes, that's it, he whispered to himself- nothing else really mattered in the end.

She was here in his heart.

And he was there in hers.

"ALWAYS" he said out loud.

Always....

*   *   *

Far from the mountains of New Guinea, a young woman stood by a large window in her home. She was alone for the moment. In her hand was a Western Union telegram, which had been just delivered. She carefully tore open the envelope and removed the message form. It only contained three laconic words, but she recognized them immediately.

Claire:
"Somewhere in Time".
Bertie.

She neatly folded the telegram again and held it firmly in her fingers. She turned and looked vacantly through the window- at nothing in particular, then gazed upward into the afternoon sky. Into the powder blue-an almost burning blue- cloudless high sky. Her face took on an intent yet wistful look. A sudden and overwhelming emotion engulfed her.

And then tears welled up in her brilliant green eyes, and began to roll slowly down, staining her face.

THE END

Hallowed Ground

Epilogue I.

".... we cannot consecrate, we cannot hallow this ground. The brave men.... who struggled here have consecrated it far above our power to add or detract. The world will little note what we say here, but it can never forget what they did here.... It is rather for us, the living, to be dedicated to the great task remaining before us.... devotion to that cause for which they gave their last full measure of devotion.... that these dead shall not have died in vain."- Abraham Lincoln.

"Death, be not proud, though some have called thee
Mighty and Dreadful,
For thou art not so.

Thou art slave to Fate, Chance, Kings,
And Desperate Men."- John Donne.

Bertie stood stock still on the edge of a jungle clearing, he and his companions awed into an absolute silence. The old man pointed to the clearing as if to say, "They are here, where my father buried them." The two now old and stately coconut trees, planted by the Natives to mark the spot in 1944, framed the head of the clearing. Bertie saw them as two pillars of honor in tribute to the fallen Americans. Here four of America's young men had reposed in the sunlit silence for seventy years. "This hallowed ground", he whispered aloud. He had expected an outpouring of elation at being taken to this place. But there was none in him. Instead, he could only say to himself "They are here. I've found them. I've found them at last." He thought only of all the wasted years, the three failed official investigations, the men who came before him to uncover the mystery of the Crew's fate: Lt. Conduit in 1945, Squadron Leader Rundle and his Searcher Team in 1947, and Lt. Belcher and his Recovery Team in 1949. They had all failed. All of the Natives just stood in silence, and so did Bertie, all of them looking at the little clearing. After 20 minutes, Bertie gave them the word to move out, and off into the jungle they filed. Bertie turned once to look back, then the jungle swallowed him up and he could no longer see place.

On their return to the river bank, they were ferried across to the village in dugout canoes. Bertie lingered at the mouth of the river where it empties into the sea. He envisioned the old man's story of the fighting that took place on this spot in 1944: the Americans had run into two Japanese soldiers at a creek one mile down the coast from here and killed them both. They then fled toward the river bank up the coast, waded the river to a sandbar contiguous with the far bank. An enemy squad of eight men caught up with them here and the shooting began, the Japanese pursuing them by crossing the river, the Americans pulling back into the nearby jungle. But they were all shot down and killed. Desperate men with little hope, Bertie thought. The dead Americans were stripped of everything and left lying where they fell. Two days later the Natives gathered them up, carried them further into the jungle, and buried them. They planted the two coconut trees that now graced the burial ground.

Bertie sat down on a large piece of driftwood on the beach. He thought of his grandfather, and of the pledge to come here to seek his dead son. Now he had at long last kept his Word. "I'm finally here, Grandpa, where he died. A little late, but I'm here." Bertie thought.

A futile search for the aircraft lay ahead. And then a march upcountry, into the interior, up steep winding ridges hemmed in by virtually impenetrable jungle, to a small village where another old man told him the stories of four more of the Crew. They had been captured and brought to an enemy counterintelligence unit near the village. There they were interrogated, tortured and executed. One grave was uncovered because a house had been built over it relatively recently. The other graves would require some meticulous searching near the village, following clues in the stories that were recounted to him. But now, with only two Rations remaining, he decided to return to the coast, twenty air miles distant to the NNE. Next morning, he arose at 0500. He was drinking his cold ration coffee when the earthquake struck. He and his field guide, Marius, ran into the open as the earth beneath them trembled and then began to shake violently. The hut they had occupied buckled. It was built close to the edge of a cliff, and he thought, if the cliff gives way we are going down into that ravine, house, chickens, roosters, the whole lot. But the trembling subsided, and no aftershocks came. His third close call since he arrived.

Because the dangers thus far had been eluded, Bertie began to become more and more confidant, but also more complacent. He believed implicitly now that his astounding luck would hold. So, it had held during the War, and was still with him, he thought. Just the week before he had survived a chance encounter with a salt water crocodile in the tidal swamps near the Verkam River. And after a grueling March to the coast through dense jungle then Sago and Mangrove swamps, he felt he could take anything. But in reality, he barely made the coast, out of food and clean water, and near exhaustion. The great physical demands of constant marching and countermarching began to take its toll on him. At home, Carolina and Claire met or spoke together every day to try to keep track of his progress. News of the earthquake shocked them, but they were helpless. The burden of worry upon them was enormous.

After three weeks of constant searching, planning, map work, early forced reveilles, nightmares, poor sleep, late nights, and wild-goose chases running down leads that ended in blind alleys, Bertie had lost weight and his stamina began to erode. He knew he badly needed several days of complete rest, but he did not have the luxury of spare time. Even after having accomplished all he could reasonably be expected to do in his quest to solve the mystery of Photo Queen, with only one planned week left, he would manage only a one-day hiatus before leaving for Kwerba and the Foja Mountains. Skipping the trip upriver on the Mamberamo to save time, he hitched a small aircraft ride with some Missionaries into Kwerba's grass airstrip. There, he asked for and got two Native escorts to the edge of the Mountains, at the edge of the Kwerba's traditional hunting grounds. Contrary to his promise not to attempt the penetration of the Fojas alone, he was dropped off in a river valley by his two escorts and began a planned four-day ascent up it to reach the rims of what he identified on satellite study as the Claw Canyons. He had sent his guide back downriver. The name he adopted for them was due to their appearance from the air as resembling the claws of a Cassowary. Then his intention was simply to do an about face and descend the way he came in three days. He carried an allowance of 14 Rations, his poncho, maps and instruments for navigation, his compass, one knife, and a few spare items of clothing including dry undergarments and socks, plus a first aid kit, and medicinal. He was embarking on a foot march into a vast trackless rain forest, with no known landmarks, no existing maps- a true unexplored wilderness of rugged terrain, cloaked in the mists of clouds swirling over and down its ridges and peaks.

On August 12th he entered the River Valley. He was never heard from after that and was never seen again. His escort of Kwerba hunters, one week later, waited at a prearranged rendezvous for three days. When Bertie failed to show up, they tried to track him up the river valley, despite their fear of those mountains. All signs pointed to him ascending the valley, but they found nothing to indicate that he returned. After a further three days of tracking, the hunters gave up and turned back. Two months' later news of his disappearance became known at the town of Kasonaweja, 70 kilometers north of Kwerba, on the Mamberamo River, below the Marine Rapids and Edi Falls. Two more weeks passed until the American Consul got the news. At his behest an Indonesian Army patrol with a few Kwerbas leading them went up the valley, climbing up into rugged terrain as far as the First Claw Canyon rim. Not a trace of Bertie was found. His final resting place would have no unique trees to set it apart from the surrounding rain forest. No searchers would ever seek to find him again. For Bertie, there would be no hallowed ground. Years would pass, and even those who mourned him would submerge his memory and go on with their lives. Why he went into the Mountains baffled everyone. If asked, he told them he just had to see them for himself, to find out what was there. No man, no human being, had ever been there. Even such a prodigious imagination as his was set on fire by the thought that he would be the first to ever set foot in them. Did he make it as far as those Canyon rims? If he had, he probably would not have been able to resist finding out what was on the floors of those Canyons. At heart, Bertie had been a true explorer his entire life, always wanting to see what was on the other side of the hill.

He had once said to Claire that when Love was lost, all that was left was Glory. In the end, even Glory eluded him.

About the same day that the Kwerba Hunting Party gave up their search for the missing Bertie, his partner in Chicago, Paul, unwrapped a thick package of papers at his home. Inside was Bertie's diary. Paul eagerly read it all the way through. In it he read the news of the American graves discovered by Bertie in the coastal jungle and far upcountry in the hills and ridges of Ankasa. He also read with growing alarm Guide Mac's cover note in broken English, telling of Bertie's foray into the Mountains. He noted the last entry in the diary, dated August 10th. After writing down his plans to penetrate the Foyas, Bertie had penciled in one final thought:

"Now 0100. Pretty hot here, even at night. Hope the Mountains are cooler. First thing when I get back- I' m going to ask Claire for that dance I've been asking her to save for me. Cheek to cheek, just like she insisted in that dream, the only way to dance.

I wonder what she'll say?"

Two Roses

(Epilogue II.) (Fifteen years later).

He had given her two roses, one white and one red, each year for two years. Each time the roses wilted and died, bent to one side, yet always remained together, still touching one another as they heeled over and drooped downward in sorrow, yet never would they part. In the third year, he purchased the roses early, in July instead of February. He would depart for the Southwest Pacific on July the fifteenth. He said to her, the first year, that to him the red rose represented he and the white rose was she. He had intended to ask her, when the two flowers finally expired, to take them and press them in an album of his writings he had given her that year. In the press of his preparations to depart, this request had been forgotten by him.

It had been fifteen years since Bertie left for New Guinea and fourteen years since he had been declared dead. He had not been heard from since the day he entered the Foja Mountains, alone. Carolina returned to her birthplace to reside with her sister, five years after a Finding of Death in his case had been issued by the court. Claire still lived with her husband in the same town. Her two eldest children were now grown and the third, young Max, was preparing to leave for college. For the two oldest, Bertie was now only a distant and vague memory. Max, of course, had no memory of him. Claire had, as was her habit, kept a strict silence. To all appearances, she no longer thought of Bertie much. He had been consigned to the past, and the Memorial Stone erected in his old family plot, ironically next to that of his Uncle, lay unadorned and unattended. The inscription on his Uncle's Memorial read "Born April 1922. Killed in Action, Southwest Pacific, September 1944." The inscription on Bertie's read "Born March 1947. Died in the Service of his Countrymen, New Guinea, August 2015."

Claire, during the emotionally staggering chore of the clearing out of his office, had taken notice of the roses. She gently wrapped them, took them home, and placed them carefully in the album. Years passed before she, one day cleaning out a closet, took the album down, finally intending to read all of the stories and poems he had written for her. She dusted it off, opened it and began to read. In these writings Bertie had poured out his feelings and thoughts and emptied the recesses of his heart. They were, he had once told her, his way of talking to her. He had always found it impossible to properly organize and divulge his true feelings to her in person. As often as not, his attempts to talk things out with her fell apart, a victim of the painful shyness that had plagued him his entire life. He had from time to time asked her earnestly to read what he had crafted for her. Claire never seemed to find the time to do so.

Now she found the effort to imbibe the writings to be an escalating, emotionally wrenching, trial. Sporadically she made her way through his heartfelt poems and stories. One evening she turned a page and came to see, once again, the two dead roses. An abrupt sob escaped her at the sight of them. Then she began to weep softly, touching them with her fingertips, placed there with her own hands so many years before. After several minutes, she at last closed the album, replaced it on the closet shelf, closed the door, and walked quickly into the next room. She began to try to busy herself with some task from her endless lists of tasks. This had been a lifelong habit of her adult life, used to shed a difficult emotion, to hide her tears. And she almost succeeded in forgetting him again, in putting his memory on that shelf with the album, and closing the door, casting what remained of him in darkness.

But this time her defensive reflex would fail. The fluid phrases of what he had written or said to her, and things she had said to him, intruded themselves into her consciousness. Try as she might, they could never be banished:

"Somewhere I will know your love, and you, mine. Somewhere in time."
"Remember me as the man who loved you".
"Save the last dance for me".
"Once, you made me smile".
"Dear Bertie, nighty-night".
"Our God must be a good God, because he has put you on this earth."

The ongoing high tide of these memories flooded into her:

"Every time we say goodbye; I die a little".
"....it will matter not how far away from you I am, nor how long ago my memories of you are.... I will see and feel your Heart light, burning bright."
"All the dearest things I know are what you are".
"Bertie, I'm sick".
"Of course, I miss you".
"I am thinking of you".
"All these dreams have perished, but one: I dream of you."

"Each time I see you, it's like the first time. It's 'just one look' all over again. Don't you see, I fall in love with you again and again and again."

"I'm proud to have known you, Claire. And I'm proud to have loved you."

"Claire, I'll never forget. I will never forget the way you made me smile."

Among these memories was the promise she had made to him so long ago: to keep him safe in her heart - Always.

And so, Claire would live out her life with Bertie somehow forever with her, the two of them together. Forgotten? Shut away in the utter dark of a closet? No, Bertie would be always being remembered by Claire- she would carry him with her, in the warm chambers of her heart. In the end, she had opened her heart to him once again. A few days after Claire placed Bertie's album back on the closet shelf, his Memorial had been cleaned up. The dry autumn leaf-fall that covered the spot had been cleared away. At the foot of the Stone lay two fresh roses, one white, one red.

In the end, she had loved him, after all.

Purity

(Epilogue III to Somewhere in Time)

".... nothing is so sacred as honor, and nothing is so loyal as love"
- adapted from "Nobility" by Alice

There exists a thing called pure love. It is uncut, unadulterated, and unconditional. There are no maybes or what ifs or how's or whys. It defies time, and thereby is ageless. It is a love that endures, and it remains unstained by circumstance, or the tragedies and triumphs two people may be subjected to in their lives. Even death itself cannot erase it nor stain its purity. Once this love is felt, it will be carried embedded in their hearts until those hearts beat no more, and then in their souls forever. It can be neither cast out nor discarded, and it will be a love that will forge a bond that can never be sundered.

And the two people who share it will always be together. Even if physically apart, they will in some way always be joined, because they are lodged in each other's hearts and souls.

In some special way, Claire and Bertie shared a pure love for each other. There were and always would be certain moments when they would find themselves looking at each other, and their eyes would soften, the gentleness in their faces conveyed an unspoken affection.

And there can be no doubt that they harbored that love to the end of their lives. Time itself failed to dim their memories of each other.

When Bertie vanished into the mist of those mountains, he would not be forgotten by her. He would be thought of in the way he wanted to be remembered: Claire would forever remember him as the man who loved her.

Appendix

Excerpts from Bertie's New Guinea Diary

20 July.

Flight Sentani to Sarmi aborted. Lost starboard engine with an oil leak. Returned to airfield, landing on one engine. Said to myself "you might as well bend over and kiss your ass goodbye. ". But it all worked out fine. Mac got us a ride to Sarmi. Driver I named Max. Actually, now Mad Max. 135 miles, needed 7 hours. Road in bad shape. Numerous bridges over creeks, rivers, ravines out due to flooding two years ago. Boards placed end on end serve as bridges. New ones under construction not finished. Just cross and pray. Crossed the Biri, Woske, Tor. Passed through Sarmi, got a look at the pier. Got a close look at two Army posts but Surat Jalan in hand. First post featured two young, apparent enlisted men, one probably an NCO. Neither in uniform. No other troops seen. He eyed me a little suspiciously asked me what I was doing here. I said I was just a tourist interested in photographing cool World War II stuff like airplanes, guns, tanks. This was the story I figured would be best believed. I had resolved never to tell them what I was really doing there. Just me being cautious. He ended passing me along to the next Post. This time I got along famously with the enlisted men in the yard, exchanging cigarettes, they seemed happy with the American version. Then a Major comes out, and he too looks me up and down with suspicion. This is because I'm dressed in my jungle utilities (khaki) and jungle boots. He complains to the Guide I look "military". We assure him I'm just a World War II nut wanting some cool photos. For good measure, to convince I'm a little looney, I tell him I want photos of dead Japanese, and does he know where there are any. He says something about Wakde. Finally, he reluctantly passes me out as ok. Picked up some bread and peanut butter in Sarmi to supplement my rations. Then we start off for the Verkam, 20 Km. away. Passed through Sijara, tiny village, thought it was bigger on map. Crossed Saborwai creek where 4 or 5 crew gunned down two Japs then fled West to the mouth of the Verkam. Finally arrived Ferkami Village at mouth of river, near sundown. Pitched tent near four huts located right at mouth of Verkam. In these huts reside four related families apparently making up a clan. Got to know all of them over next three weeks. With indefatigable Guide Marius, Mac having returned to Sentani and Wamena on business with Mad Max. First person I must mention is Tracea, 17 years old, the go to gal if you need food, coffee, laundry. I call her Tracey. Kid has aspirations on being a nurse and wants to go to college in Jayapura. Family does not have the resources for this, however. When I leave, I'm going to give her what I can in the way of money. We bathe in an enclosure made of tin sidings with buckets of well water. My tent big enough for me and gear. In downpours must close up both netting and outer cover, which induces a sweat bath. My sleeping mat loaned to me by Marius does little to alleviate the hard ground effects, it's just a quarter inch hard straw mat. Hips, back, and my old broken ribs plague me. Frequent awakenings during the night to shift side to side or awakened by strange noises. Habitual

Reveille for me is 0500. Get trousers and boots on, sit outside with my morning Ration, an MRE. These are actually not bad. I give away chiclets and any candy to the kids. Then personal hygiene. The Head is any secluded spot you can find. The little E-Tool I brought comes in handy. Morning ritual of my personal meds plus malaria pill. Then at about 0800 Tracey has boiled water for coffee for all Hands. No coffee pots are used, instead ground coffee and raw sugar are stirred into the boiled water. Fried plantains are served. Rest of the days are marching and counter marching through the swamp forests or jungle in search of the aircraft or graves. Peter Kallum, 62 years old, is the first to offer information. I asked no leading question, nor did I give any information. Simply asked if anyone knew about any fighting between Americans and Japanese in vicinity of village. Then I was silent letting them tell any stories.

They began talking about the fighting at Wakde and Maffin Bay. When they were finished, I asked about anything closer to the village. The next story was about an aircraft which bombed and sank a Japanese ship of unknown type off the coast, sinking it, but hit by AAA the plane crashed into the sea 500 yards off the coast. They said there were no survivors. I then asked for fighting right around the village or just up the coast. That was the ticket.

Peter's father told him about the fighting between part of the crew and the Japs at the mouth of the river. His father told him the Americans were attempting to cross the river mouth from east to West Bank wading to a sand bar contiguous to the West Bank (Note: this sandbar is almost certainly the "island in the mouth of the Verkam" alluded to by Rundle in 1947 as possibly containing some remains. Rundle stated he was sending his Searcher Team to check it out, but no further report is extant on what they may have found there). Once there, the Japanese caught up to them and began shooting at them from the East Bank. Some or all of the Americans, whether wounded or not is unclear, made it to the tree line, but the Japs pursued them into the jungle and killed them all. Apparently, they were left where they fell, and a day or two later the Natives gathered up the dead and buried them deeper in the jungle. They then planted two coconut trees at the graves site to mark them. I asked them specifically whether any Americans were killed on the sand bar. Peter categorically said all were killed in the jungle beyond.

The next morning, we waded the river at low tide and Peter led us up the beach to a point just shy of Cape Verkam, where we struck off into the jungle, emerging briefly at a single large hut which my guide explained as a hunter's camp. We reentered the jungle and wound our way along a trail not used for some time, as Johanne our chief machete man had to cut a way through. We crossed a short log bridge over a swampy area. I lost my balance and fell in. Unhurt but embarrassed, I was picked up by two of the boys and we waded out of the mire. Eventually we emerged in front of two tall and old coconut trees, sort of framing a large open spot about 5x8 yards in area that was shown to me as the burial spot. The two trees were older as indicated by being encased for a distance upward by vines. I was not elated as I thought I would be. We were all silent. I whispered my single thought, "They are here. I found them. Found them at last. This is hallowed ground". It was for me an emotional moment. The coordinates of this spot: Lat. 1Deg48'16"S.- Long. 138Deg40'49"E. We then returned by a different and easier, shorter route by turning to starboard onto an old, overgrown dirt road which led us to the Verkam just fifty yards to the South of the mouth. Because it was high tide, Canoes then ferried us back to the East Bank. It was sunset now.

When I first stepped onto the East Bank the day before, near dusk, I was engulfed in emotion, thinking of my Grandfather and my pledge to him to come to this place, where his son died. I made that promise in 1974, having returned from my own overseas service. I was fit then and knew the jungle. Much to my shame and regret I never went. Ironically, I had shown my Grandfather a map and put my finger on a place called Sarmi, telling him I thought they may have ditched there along the coast. I now felt, at least, I had redeemed my Word to him. Tears would well up in my eyes at that moment, and again when I had a last look before I left. Evening Nautical Twilight was ending by the time I walked back into the clan compound.

21 July.

Checking out rumor of place up country a little where a Native informant says the wreck of PQ is. He says he saw the tail section upended sticking out of the ground. Walked about three KM. by road to South then cut off into trail to our right, that is, West. Searched all morning and into afternoon. Swamp forest is wet and loaded with leeches, and the point men cut trail for the rest of us. Operating now on the East bank of the River. From Belcher's search in 1949 we know he looked for wreck on the West Bank. BUT it is pointed out to me that the River changed its course in 1963, moving to the WEST. Remnant of Old River course is pointed out to me near the bridge. So, we are actually searching the West Bank of the Old River- the EAST BANK of the New River. Came up empty EXCEPT for a piece of rusted engine cowling half buried in the dirt. And in this same area the boys find a 500-lb. bomb split longitudinally with an intact fuse cap lying next to it. Took photos of this. No tail section found. Wild goose chase. So now I know some Native stories are going to be exaggerated, or there might be nothing to them at all. But I also know I've got to follow up each lead, even if some of them end up in blind alleys. Good weather with a sea breeze keeps Mosquitos away for now, at least on the coast next to camp. The swamps are a different story.

22 July.

Another early call and March south to and into the "Parrot's Beak" north of the bridge. Same tangled swamp forest-jungle mix we've been slogging through on our previous forays. Oppressive, humid heat. Leeches in abundance. Stop to burn them off with a cigarette every so often. That leaves sores on my arms, so I treat them with mupirocin ointment 2%, and it works like a charm. Last thing you want are chronic nonhealing tropical ulcers. They cling to my boots too. But they can't find a way in- I've got 'em laced up tight. We never quite make it to the river bank on any of these searches. That's because the swampy terrain along those banks are known crocodile haunts. Natives shy away from them. These are salt-water crocs, inhabiting these tidal, mangrove swamps, reputedly the most aggressive of their species. Mangrove swamps are also pure hell to try to penetrate. The mangroves are thorny and their roots extending underwater in the swamp canals are treacherous. Dry land hard to come by. Lucky if you can make 100 yards an hour in this stuff.

23 July.

Walked South a little further than we did two days ago, then cut off road and this time cut trail moving west toward the river. Fruitless search. Made our way to bridge, then returned to Ferkami. Before we did, I ventured on the road of the Parrot's Beak, as I call it, to check on the mystery object- it turns out to a bulldozer in an old logging area. Before we were through, we searched the Parrot's Beak completely on daily patrols with few results.

24 July.

Tip from a Native I call Rusty. Further up from our search area he claims many pieces of an aircraft. So, we set out early and the further we go, the more astounded I become. Could Harms have flown this far? It turns out we leave the road 16 KM South of Ferkami!!! This area is only about six miles to the NNW of Amsira. We leave the logging road, and almost immediately the jungle trail descends abruptly down a precipitous, muddy slope to a steep-banked swamp canal. It's a good twenty-foot drop into the canal. The muddy trail follows the bank south, then west leading to

a crude footbridge over the canal, really just a big tree felled across the canal. Rusty says he ran across these pieces deep in the jungle two months ago. So, we follow him in, again moving more or less west towards the river, and it's a long walk, recutting the trail as we go. Crossed that single log bridge over a deep swamp canal. The log is thirty feet long, and it's a twenty foot drop below. The tree trunk is much wider on this one, but as I gingerly cross I notice a single crocodile eyeballing me, his long snout and red eyes staring at me. Waiting for me to fall in, I guess. But this time I make it. Despite almost losing my balance, steadied up by my canteen boy, Mickey and Guide Marius. It was a close call. I was actually falling. Twenty feet down into that slime. A couple of seconds more and....
The walk through the jungle is tough, circuitous, and it wears me down. Lots of blow downs across the old trail. Lot of mud popping up frequently, especially nearer the River where the thick jungle gives way to swamp- Forest. Since the trail hasn't been used in a few months, the point men wield machetes, cutting trail practically all the way. On the map I note our route follows a sort of inverted V of several Klicks. We cut our way North for 4 Klicks, then turn left and strike off to the Southwest, parallel to the Verkam. At the spot at long last are several twisted, rusting, unidentifiable pieces. One piece they dig out of the ground is an engine cowling with part of a propeller attached. Only two bent blades, and it seems too small for a B-24. Downpour catches us. The Natives quickly use palm fronds to make a roof over me, but I'm soaked anyway before it is finished. My main man is Mickey, Tracy's brother, who carries my canteen and sticks with me like glue. Mickey goes with me as I strike off alone to the North and then a hair East towards the River loops, I named "The EKG Loops" because they look like the PQRST waves of an EKG, running from the South to North. The rest of the patrol are busy digging up pieces of metal debris. I'm trying to visualize the crash-landing axis of aircraft as the ship descends parallel to the long axis of the River. If this debris is PQ, Harms will parallel the River from NNE to SSW and try to put it down closer to the

River. He should have been able to see the River as a kind of dull silver ribbon of snakelike loops in the almost full moon, off his port quarter bearing 105 degrees (actually a waxing gibbous moon on the night of <u>30 September</u>). I can only advance about 75 yards due to heavier undergrowth and swampy terrain, and I have lost sight of the rest of the Party. So, we return following a compass back azimuth, or a reciprocal course as in air or water navigation. Mickey and the rest now call me Tuan James, a Malay word in their language which means "Lord". We return to Ferkami, me arriving just tapped out. We covered a total of 30 Km on the logging road, down and back, and another 10 in the jungle. I turn in early. But I wake up several times. Two Head calls. The Head is in the brush behind the beach. Or down by the water. You've got to take care walking down to the water as the beach is in places choked with debris and driftwood. Nightly rains begin, so I button up in the tent, bathed in sweat. Tracy gathers my laundry to hand wash. These good people of Ferkami treated me with the utmost deference. They never asked me for anything in return, and they went out with me day after day to search without complaint. They took no rest breaks in our passage through the jungles and swamps, and seldom took even a sip of water. I was assured by Peter even after I left, they would continue the search for the aircraft. And they never asked me for a red cent. I had Marius pay them something before we left. I gave a little money to Tracy and Mickey personally. I think my coming here is a big deal for these people. I don't believe any of them, either in Ferkami or Ankasa has ever seen an American. They immediately adopted a sense that this was a Mission of some importance and turned to with enthusiasm to help me search. And in both places, they displayed instant hospitality to me, a complete stranger, falling into their laps unannounced. The deference they showed me was a pleasant surprise, and a little embarrassing maybe to an egalitarian-minded Yankee. Nevertheless, you must take up the mantle of leadership the Natives give you and not disappoint them.

Became the village Doctor, after Marius reveals my profession. The locals approach me one at a time. A sick infant with a viral syndrome, two young adults with bronchitis, one man with an eczematous rash. My chief machete man, Johannes, has a ureteral stone and dehydration. He also has acquired a dependence on Betel Nut. Tracy comes down with sinusitis and bronchitis. I notice she's trying out Betel Nut, so I forbid her to use it, and she stops immediately. With Johannes I have proscribed coffee until he passes the stone, and he pours out the coffee in the cup quickly into the dirt. I think "Talk about following Doctor's Orders!" These people are the epitome of compliance. I was shocked by their immediate actions to satisfy my wishes. Fortunately, 1 have brought along an ample supply of antibiotics and Aleve and Tylenol. I am quite impressed by the rapidity of my new patient's recovery- the colds and coughs disappear in just a few days. My theory is that the bacteria here have never come into contact with antibiotics- to these organisms the meds are like nuclear weapons. Not a very scientific hypothesis. But it seems the Natives now view me in awe as some sort of miracle worker, and I have instantly gained a reputation as a super-sorcerer in their eyes. Add that to my other title, Tuan (Lord) James. Johannes reports for duty the next day, says he is cured.

25-26 July.

Out searching, again north of the bridge in the upper Parrot's Beak. Both during Conduit's investigation with 2 Australian War Crimes outfit in 1945, and Rundle's effort in 1947 the location of the wreck is invariably called somewhere on the "upper reaches of the Verkam"- even the Jap. testimony refers to the place as such. Without my prompting, the natives, when asked, said the maddening magic words: "upper reaches". Our efforts now proved fruitless. My own study of close-in satellite photos led me to guess the plane was to be found SOUTH of the Parrot's Beak near some loops in the river I called (from north to south) the Keyhole, the First Tee, and the

Corner Pocket. My favored spot was at the base of the First Tee, on the West Bank of the new river. Learning of the change of course in the river in 1963 changed my thinking only in moving the estimated spot to the east of the new river and to the west of the old river. Then another Native came to us with an intriguing story: his grandmother found the wreck with the pilot dead inside and she and others then buried him 25 yards from the nose of the plane and planted flowers on the grave. This prompted a search to the north of the bridge and the discovery of what I called the Flower Garden, three small flowers sprouting out of the ground. My instinct was to dig up both the Flower Garden and the Coconut Grove, but the natives would not dig and advised against it. So, the idea was dropped. In any case no trace of the plane was found near the Garden. And digging is probably best left to the forensic boys at DOD. Not to mention I may have ended up cooling my heels in an Indonesian Army prison. Besides my time was growing short, and I felt we must go to Amsira in search of Rafael and Julian. The wreck itself was useless to us, unless we could prove Harms remained at the controls after his men bailed out and died in the crash. Then DOD would be compelled to go in. After all it was the crew's remains that counted- get them home.

- Peculiar guy shows up suddenly on track out of Ferkami, accosts me with a falsetto hail fellow well met persona. Flashes a fake smile showing teeth dis colored red with Betelnut. I shake loose from him. He tries to latch on again. So, I sarcastically ask him if anybody ever told him he looks like a Zombie with those teeth. But that late afternoon he shows up in Ferkami. Sits next to me and asks in good English "What are you doing here" and "How long are you going to be here". I give him no clear answer then I ask him what his line of work is, where is he from etc. He simply answers Yes to every question. No more good English? This guy is an Army spy or informer, sent by the Major who was so suspicious of me in Sarmi. But eventually he departs, and we are troubled no more. My "cover story" of being a World War Two nut looking for good pictures holds up. The Major in Sarmi was

- suspicious of me, eyeing my khaki field utilities and jungle boots- I guess I looked too "military" to him. As a footnote, on our journey to Amsira via the Orai route- I take note of three large Army posts on the bend of the Orai with unit names and total about a reinforced battalion size. Puzzles me that these all new facilities, but no vehicles and not a single soldier in sight, not even a sentry on the gates. In fact, the first post we stopped into near Sarmi to obtain the Surat Jalan, only two men in the office, none seen in barracks area. One a junior NCO type reticent and suspicious. His weapon is lying carelessly on the floor at the foot of an empty rifle rack. Neither of them is in uniform. At the next stop, a small admin post in Sarmi, got along well with the dozen troopers I met. Then Major Suspicious came out. I repeat for his benefit my cover story of World War II maniac looking for cool stuff to snap pictures of. Passed out American cigarettes to any enlisted men around, to universal "oohs and ahhhs". But he let us go on. Never did get a written Surat Jalan.

A word on this Betel-Nut business. Everyone who uses the stuff keeps a betel nut sack attached to him. They gather a type of seaweed, pound it into a fine powder and use it with the betelnut. It is this mixture that gives the user red teeth.

27 July.

Departed Ferkami, headed to Amsira. Goodbyes always tough. Here the people were so good to me, so hospitable, asking for nothing in return. They searched with me day after day without complaint, they provided food, they even worried about me to the point of moving my tent in much closer to their homes. They all gathered in the compound to say goodbye. My number one boy, Mickey, tapped his heart with his hand several times as we parted, trying to tell me he will never forget me. His sister Tracy asked after me for days afterward. Shaking hands with Peter Kallum, I had to fight to control my emotions. At least I instructed the Guide to pay them a fair amount. Peter indicated to me through hand signals he would carry on the quest for the aircraft. As I walked away all I could manage was a big wave of my cap. Who knows whether I will ever see them again?

Ahead lay a hard trail to Amsira. Mad Max could only take us partway on the dirt road paralleling the Orai River. Ahead lay swamp forest then heavy jungle, with only a narrow single track with impenetrable jungle on either side, steep hills up which the narrowing trail wound inexorably toward Amsira. The climbing, twisting trail was very hard on my legs, which began to ache before outright pain set in in the muscles. This necessitated frequent stops to rest them. My companions were Mr. Daber, a retired Army officer, and Marius Revideso, my guide throughout the whole search. Mac Wasage was off on other business. My two compatriots were unflagging in their trek and showed constant concern for me, their aging partner. Track gets ever steeper as we toil upward, each successive ridge higher than the last. A few huts begin to appear, set back in the jungle, with pilings to support them, as they are built into the slopes. The track narrows here, and there are spots with sheer drops of forty feet or more, bottoming out in languid jungle watercourses. Water looks deep, hope I don't lose balance here- the fall alone would cripple you. A few Natives have passed us on the trail, so our presence has been revealed to the villagers. Modern form of the old jungle telegraph- announcing the imminent arrival of a tall white guy. I'm sure I'm the only one of those within 200 miles. In fact, I am almost certainly the first American they have laid eyes on. Last ridge a bitter struggle to get up, leg muscles burning now- lactic acid in the tissue. At a final rest stop, time to check the map. Orient the map to the compass.

We are on a magnetic Azimuth of 262 degrees, almost due West. Eyeing the track, it looks like it veers to the Southwest as it winds upward. On the 1944 map the first Ville is named Tulitimi. I check with Marius and Daber, but they never heard that name. Recent Indonesian maps, I suddenly recall, call the place Tolitimi. My boys shake their heads- no, Tuan, says Marius, doesn't ring a bell with us. Time to saddle up and move out, get up this next ridge, now inclined at a cruel angle. Don't know it yet, but this turns out to be the final push over the top and we emerge suddenly onto a plateau. Just down the trail 20 yards is a kind of compound off to the right. We waked into it, unsteadily, feeling tipsy as my exhaustion overcame me. An older man seemingly materialized out of thin air, giving me an orange plastic chair, which I gratefully accepted, and I sat down heavily after shedding my pack and pistol belt. With everyone seated, Marius made the introductions. Daber and Marius communicated with the man in Indonesian. I already was aware of the plethora of tribal languages inundating the entire island of New Guinea, having studied a language map of Western New Guinea. Mac had told me in Sentani that the tribes could never talk to one another if they did not use the idiom of Indonesia. Thus, I thought, another nail in the coffin of Papuan independence.

We learn we are short of Amsira in a village called Ankasa. Old man here tells us stories over two days. Nightfall fast approaching. Amsira still more than two miles over steep ridges away. Significantly Amsira is called the "new village". I elect to sleep on the portico of the hut, my companions inside. Hut situated on a cliff on the edge of a ravine. Old man tells us his father told him a captured American was brought here, delivered to the Tora Kikan. He says this first prisoner was the "pilot", and the villagers had heard of the crashed plane and intended to help him, but he was captured before they could do anything. He was killed by the Japs and was buried. He knows where the grave is, because a house was built over it much later. He gives the name of Abinasan as the Jap in charge of Tora Kikan. Significantly he uses the term Tora Kikan without me having mentioned it to him.

He then related the story of yet another prisoner. He says the single prisoner is invited to a Jap celebration or "party" by one of the Jap officers, but after a time the other officers become angry and take the American away and kill him. This prisoner would be Catlin, captured much later than the others, towards the end of October. His story that Catlin was brought in much later than the others fits the facts. The old man does not know where the American is buried, but there is a sort of Jap cemetery, he says, but far from Amsira. The old man's wife during the evening of conversation brings out an old Jap mess kit, then an American canteen, the old metal kind, and an American mess kit with a spoon, right out of 1945. The canteen is being used to heat something up and I recognize it almost at once. Then she trots out the mess kit. I ask where she got the stuff, but all she knows her husband's father gave him the things. We eventually turn in. Tough to get any continuous sleep- damn mosquitos are attacking in swarms. So, I douse myself with repellant on the skin and permethrin onto my clothing, a T-shirt and what my brother calls tighty-whiteys. Finally, dripping with bug poison, I drift off. Awakened q hour to shift positions, the old broken ribs and sore knee giving me fits. These afflictions will always force me to remember the night I got them, so many years ago- the blackest of nights on a jungle trail. Even my peerless point man, with the night vision of a cat, was blinded. Entire patrol went right over the unseen cliff. Still shake my head at the sight of us, a bunch of limping, cursing Marines, filing back into the Firebase next day.

28 July.

The roosters begin crowing at about 0500 with the Beginning of Morning Nautical Twilight. I am drinking cold ration coffee from my next to last MRE. We are all seated on the portico at about 0700 when an earthquake hits shaking the house violently. We run into the open in front of the hut, the tremor lasts 15-20 seconds then subsides. I look anxiously at the adjacent ravine, thinking with the next tremor we are all going down into it, chickens, roosters, house and all. But no more tremors come. Later, I discover the epicenter for this was just to the ESE of Kwerba on the edge of the Foya Mountains, and this where I was headed when the PQ investigation was wrapped up. 7.2 on the scale. I imagine the rock slides triggered in the Foyas. Luck of the draw still with me. Daber sat near the edge of the cliff, apparently calm, through the tremor. Marius tells me we should return to Sarmi then Sentani. But we will pump the old man for more information first. The reason for returning is simple- we've been through the wringer in these jungle marches and we've still got a 20 mile walk down the steep ridges then through jungle, swamp forest, and swamps back to the coast. It's going to take us two days. It is more like thirty miles if we follow the Bend of the Orai, instead of transiting the jungle. And I have only one Ration left. To check out all the stories and rumors would take a week or more. And I've even resolved to skip the Foyas and get home. Without the MREs I will lose more than the eight lbs. I've lost already on just one Ration per day. I've supplemented this with bread and peanut butter and hard-boiled eggs, but the limited calorie intake just can't keep up with the huge number I burn up every day. Did try Sago, a gummy substance that is virtually tasteless. Distances here are always described by the Natives as nearby when in fact the places are far apart connected by rugged terrain. If the destination is called far by Marius, then it's going to be a long haul.

The old man now tells us his father heard two men survived a crashed plane along the "upper Verkam"(there's that phrase again), and the natives up here wanted to help them. Then he said one of them was "black". This was later clarified as one of them being swarthy (Rafael? he was Puerto Rican). But the Police Boys grabbed them (on separate days, just the way the Japs described it) and he said they were brought to the Tora Kikan. So, they were killed but he doesn't know where they were buried. My guess now, collating all these stories is they, Catlin, Rafael, Julian, and possibly Harms are all buried around Ankasa. When Marius and Mac return here, I am going to tell them to concentrate on grave sites. The grave with house built over it is going to be one site DOD must excavate.

Marius says the natives won't mind it a bit. If all this pans out, the Coconut Grove and Ankasa, we may hit pay dirt.

29 -30 July.

Rough, even brutal, return March to the coast to rendezvous with Mad Max. Me, Daber, and Marius. Short descriptions of the two days inserted here from emails I sent, brief recounting of our "march to the sea". It was my own doing. Thinking shortcut, instead of going all along the Bend of the Orai, I figured we could cut 10 miles from the journey by striking off into the jungle along a trail I spotted ion the way up. Should have known better- trail turns into no more than a trace, then vanishes in the thickest jungle I've ever seen. All this because Mad Max can't make it to a rendezvous point West of Marareno to pick us up. So, we wear ourselves out cutting trail with machetes. Jungle only lasts 4 miles or so, but it takes us 5 hours to cut our way through. The green hell gives way to Sago then Mangrove Swamp as we near the coast. Had to keep telling myself just put one foot in front of the other and keep going. By the time we hit the beach I'm without food for 13 hours and all I've got left to drink is swamp water, albeit filtered and purified with special tablets. After bathing in the ocean, the remaining leeches fall off, I strip off all my filthy clothes. We hand our machetes to a couple of gawking kids to climb up the coconut trees and throws down some green coconuts. The juice is sweet and seems like nectar from heaven, wiping out my hypoglycemic state. One more footnote: Mac tells me in Sentani that the Indonesian Army has a museum in which one exhibit is a collection of AMERICAN DOG TAGS. I instruct him to get me a list of names and serial numbers on those tags.

August 1.

Have heard a couple of newspapers and TV stations are interested in the story of this Expedition. We will wait to see if any interviews come our way. Map work is painstaking. Worked on it two hours last (Sunday) night. Must draft orders for guides to give them specific missions and objectives but encourage them to also use their own instincts and initiative. Will wait for meeting with Paul- funding is next paramount object to accomplish. And we must frame our strategy. Clarify overall Mission: bring as many of Crew back as possible, then see they are all buried in Arlington under a common memorial stone listing entire crew as if they were all there.

Reviewed Kallum's story: his father tells him of the fighting at the mouth of the River. Begins with four Americans crossing sand bar, Japs appear on East bank, shooting begins, Americans make the jungle tree line, Japs pursue and kill them all in the jungle beyond, on the West Bank. Japs leave them where they fall. Few days later Natives gather them and take them deeper into jungle and bury them, planting two coconut trees to mark spot.

1. Story fits Jap testimony in 1945 that they killed four of crew, but they say they buried them on the spot. Fighting is said by Japs to occur at the Verkam. Japs likely lied about burying them, not known to take the trouble to bury enemy dead. Both Native and Jap accounts place number of U.S. Dead at four. It is not known why Australian investigators did not follow up the Jap. Account- i.e., take us to the spot and show us where the graves are.

2. Story fits in with Rundle's sending his team in 1947 to search "island in the mouth of the Verkam". That is the sand bar. He probably hears from some Native tip on the fighting there, but team finds nothing- if they had found remains Rundle would have reported it, yet he is silent on results.

3. Story of coconut trees- two old and tall trees are observed to frame the clearing where graves are said to be. Trees are old, indicated by dense vines encasing them, and by their height.

4. Story is detailed.

All of the above go to the veracity of the Native testimony as recounted by Peter Kallum. My overall impression is the account is truthful.

Reviewed old man's stories in Ankasa:

1. Father tells him village hears of a crashed American plane down on the Verkam. Some of the villagers go down intending to help and aid crewmen to get back to U.S. Base to the East. But the Japs capture the pilot and bring him here to Ankasa and kill him. Where was he buried, I ask? His grave had a house built over it sometime later. I ask if the occupants will be upset about tearing up their floor to get at the grave. He says no.

2. After the pilot, two other Americans are captured, one white and the other a darker complexion. They are brought to Amsira on different days, first the white man, then the other man. In this recounting he lays great emphasis on the desire or perhaps attempts of the villagers to help these two prisoners to somehow get to the American lines. He repeats this part of the story a few times. They are both brought to Ankasa and killed. He does not know where their graves are.

3. Much later, another American is brought here. A Jap. Officer takes him to a "party" or celebration. There, the other officers see this and get angry, seize the American, take him into the jungle and kill him. Site of his grave is not known. But there is a Jap. Cemetery in Amsira, maybe he is there, the old man says.

4. Next day, the old man elaborates- he says the TORA-KIKAN killed the Americans. His use of this term, the name of the Japanese counterintelligence and espionage unit attached to their 36th Division, catches my attention immediately. The camp for this outfit is near Ankasa, according to the old man.

Impressions:

1. His contention that the villagers wished to help the crew is unlikely. All captured crew were taken by the Police Boys, Papuan collaborators, led by Indonesians. This first story, of the pilot, adds a fourth prisoner we were unaware of. It accounts for the "missing man" when we add up the casualties in the various fights by the mouth of the River. If it was Harms, then he crash landed the plane after his men all bailed out. There may be one other man not accounted for in the Japanese testimony, and if so that man may still be in the wreck.

2. The story of the next two men, brought in separately on different days fits the fact that Rafael and Julian were captured on different days, 2-3 days apart. His characterization of Rafael as a man of swarthy complexion fits with the copilot's Puerto Rican ethnicity. His insistence on the villager's motives to help these two prisoners may be significant if the Japanese account of their escape and recapture toward the end of October is true. Heretofore we have regarded the escape story to be a Japanese fabrication. Thus, the escape episode needs to be reexamined by future probing of the old man in a careful way so as to not allude to the escape, letting him elaborate villager efforts on his own.

3. His account of the last captive fits in with Catlin's capture near the end of October, as being much later than the others. The "party" incident does not seem far-fetched if consideration is given to the typical behavior of the Japanese officers of that era. Cut off, starving, disease ridden, the 36th's officers get stoked up with some Saki, and become at first playful then belligerent. It fits their attitudes towards prisoners, in this case bringing Catlin out as an object of curiosity then an object of their hatred.

4. His out of blue mention of TORA-KIKAN, not just once but three times, is telling. He could not know that I was thoroughly familiar with that infamous unit. (My term for them was Murder Incorporated.).

Printed in Dunstable, United Kingdom